Kissing Tales

Acknowledgements

I dedicate this novel to the family and friends who just refused to give up on me no matter how easy I made it too just do so. Glory to God to the highest for all that you do in the lives of the ones I love and mine. I have been difficult at times I know it and you are still your there. Thank you.

My little brother "Cheff" Rest easy young soldier. I love you. Face, I will see you soon. Cheonett, thanks cousin for being ore like my twin sister more than anything. Wilfred for being the first I could call. Berlla, you taught me, it is ok to go at things your way if you go at things. Emily my first kiss in kindergarten of Florence Ave school in Miss Tapioca's class 1990 in Irvington, NJ. Nikki, the world is a darker place without your light hold a spot for me love. Nina, one of us must write this stuff down cousin lol. Sunny my overprotective little cousin thank you twin. To my whole entire MADE team.

Alorah, girl you are my inspiration and life, and you always will be, know that please. Mr. Pecker keep one on ice for me up there will you lol. Jennifer my great editor and supporter who seems to be editing my whole entire life in ways to hard not to notice, love you for being dedicated to family and the love you put into this.

My gratitude is limitless to porn industry, who has kept my mind super active and my innovations especially nasty. All the wonderful ladies to self-proclaimed whores who rode this wave and bends I dished out leading up to this. The fellas who push them into my bed, nice going. To all the voyeurs and swingers in the world you rock! All the honest men out there, no not you I said honest SMH. To the Caribbean and Latin community Major, Brazy, Ghost, Spazz,nahn-man, power, Moni, Raxx and showtime my brother from another mother, thank you for always being there when shit gets real. TT you keep the jewels of my heart protected, salute you lady. As time goes by, I realize all the people, places and things that have made good and valuable impacts on my life. I may have missed a few this time but this only the beginning. I will get you all in I promise. Just stay tuned…. I love you all.

Prologue

For as long as I could remember I have been interested in everything sex. Maybe it was the intrigue of women, then to find out all the wonderful things I could do with them, got it going in my mind. Many are going to assume my interest in sex or fucking are just the same as any others, right? Well, you're wrong there are far too many versions of what people like or are aroused by. That is what makes it so great. I make it easy to be just as naughty and nasty as you like. No holds bars, (unless that is your thing). Straight dirty talking, cum squirting, toe cracking good freaking. Like my parents, many shield their children from sex like drugs. But the mind gets curious and how long do you really think it will be till the cats out of the box or the cock in the box? Do not blush these are questions we have all asked ourselves or a friend in privacy.

I remember my first sex experience like it was yesterday. My parents rented out a basement bedroom to a very cool young couple down on their luck from our church. This was my childhood home back in Irvington NJ. I may have been about 11 or maybe 12 years old. Do not worry I will use different names in case you guys do not want yours out there, contact me after you read this if you decided otherwise. Anyway, Mike and Onna were super cool. Mike was a great guy with dark skin between 280 and 300 lbs. Built like a linebacker off the Eagles, a real beast. But he was soft spoken and played the guitar at church and even when he moved in, he kept all of us dancing. By all of us that would be me and my siblings. There was 6 in total. Myself 1 kid brother all the rest sisters. Onna was a beautiful brown skin chick bright eye that demanded your attention. She was 5.5 140 to 150 lbs. She had wide hips and a large pair of tits, that I always seem to look at no matter where I saw them while I was growing up. Her full figure at her height rally stood out to me even back then. She was nice and easy on the eyes. Her features just made a young boy's mind wonder so deeply. Everything from her smile and shake in her walk was provocative to me. Onna was part of the choir and had a beautiful voice, together they made it easy to like them. They were Haitian like us and helped us a lot with understanding the cultural differences.

Once I was sick and home from school, my parents of course off to work, siblings at their school so I was home alone. "PERFECT" I used the 1st day of my 3 days off to be in place and things forbidden when parents and tattle tale sisters were home. I do not really know what I was looking for or hoping to find till it happened I fell upon my first dirty magazine. I just could not believe how perfect this really was. My father, I assumed had really gone the distance to keep it from us all. Maybe even mom may have not known it to be there either, because it was in a cabinet over the refrigerator. Made to keep things from people under seven foot from reaching, without assistance from a step ladder, like I had used anyway.

Once on the top step I sat on top of my parent's new fridge and slowly opened the possibly spider filled cabinet, no spiders but what there was a small revolver that caught a glint of light. It was almost hypnotizing. My hand was creeping towards it almost out of my control. My parents had a strict, no guns rule not even toy ones were allowed in our house. Now to see a real one.

The glint of the gun had faded to a blur as I went tunnel vision on those pretty set of naked boobs. The best-looking boobs ever and there naked on the front cover of what looked like a book or magazine. I was a lot more reluctant to move and grab this object though. But eventually I did, and I have been different since. I know it had to be just like the ones from the TV shows "Just like" boobs I could not believe it... By the time I had found this magazine I had only four hours left to understand and what this was.

Every single page had high resolution photos of white and black woman showing parts of their bodies I did not know existed. The nipples on the boobs looked far more interesting on a woman compared to mine and why did the guy seem to want to eat them? In these photos the guys were eating the girl's "pussy" as the story explained in the margins "and she loved sucking his cock at the same time." If I had not read this myself, I would not have believed such a thing. All the hype about having a girlfriend changed almost immediately. "69's it was about "69."

The story continued "She slammed her ass into my hips and screamed in pleasures" It was like reading direction to making a good cake. Then I found myself being I mean really excited at the pictures of penetration "hard cock in her cunt", the way it was written. Next thing I knew I was touching myself making an o with my hand to make a pretend "pussy" so my "cock" could go into feel what this guy explained as "so amazing and moist." No moisture from her but the pressure felt really good and when I went up and down even better.

How could it have taken so long for me to discover. Two hours left although I had plenty of time, I figured I was only on page eleven. Some of the words where difficult and new not to mention the distraction that came from the glossy pictures. Every page seemed to be better than the last one and this had to be the greatest discovery since milk and cookies. Right, I mean it had to be.

But mid through there was a crunching of the gravel in our driveway Someone was home. I threw the magazine back in the cabinet like it was hot at first then thought better of it, I tried to put it back exactly as it was before. I heard the car door close at the same time as I shut the cabinet doors which made me jump a little like I had shut them loud enough for the approaching person to hear. I scurried down the short ladder laid it down on its side and released the lock to shove the legs quietly as possible. Just as I put it back under the leaking patch my dad had been working on the night before in the living room the back door was being unlocked and pushed opened. Just then I looked down and realized I had a tent in the front of my shorts. I ran to the sink pretending to be doing the dishes by the time the humming of Onna's melody got to my ears. "Hey honey, are you feeling better" she asked. My heart still beating the hardest ever. "Yah almost", croaked out just leaking over my shoulder in time to see her bent over into the exact fridge I had spent the best hours of my life, and looking at her in that position made my tent harder to hide, it was painful almost. Once she was out of sight my heartbeat began to go back to normal, but the thoughts and pictures remained in my mind and the rage in my boner was relentless. When I showered and made the "O" and stuck my Cock" in it over and over that it felt like I was transforming into a monster, under the showers spray. I saw stars and I may have heard a loud bang. If I could remember clearly, I thought maybe I broke something. But boy did it feel good and relieving overall. The stressed thoughts and spent up energy feeding it, had all been spent and washed down the drain. "I love you O".

That is when it all stared for me the obsession with sex. So, for my fans and admires. I love it all. Rough sex is my favorite. MILFS, young but legal, white girls but do not discriminate, high heels, and pumps the come fuck me style, long hair and short. Size does not make a difference as long as the curves stand out and yes eating ass is good for everyone's health. I will not be kissing and telling, well not their real name anyway in my stories. I love the apple bottom love from all the ladies out there. Kissing is my thing if I know my dick was the last one in your mouth for the past hour or so. Shout out to Miss D for being the only woman who could make me cum with her mouth, I will be to see you soon.

A voyeur is someone who likes to look and watch rather than really get physically involved in the activities he or she is watching. There is a power executed in it for me. The kinkier the better. Loud sound like spanking, screaming moans, and my personal favorite direct comments really get me off. I am pretty well hung so when I find a tight pussy girl that really drips and squirts with the deep strokes I promise to deliver, it is a great thing. Watching is awesome to.

Writing all these stories puts me right in the room with you. Sex is a more open subject now compared to the era I was growing up in, but it is still in some ways protected and guarded amongst adults who do it every single day. Let us not be too shy now it is made for us to enjoy no matter who you are.

That night all I could think of was the wonderful light blue green veins that appeared under the skin of the white women big firm breast and the wet mouths of the black ones kept reappearing in my mind. The words "cunt, Cock Fuck me and deeper stung my mental to no end. There where over 300 pages according to the cover, that had yet to be explored. I was almost tempted to try to get to them that night but thought better of it. I avoided my siblings and parents almost embarrassed by my newly discovered treasure. Even my brother would not be told about this one and at that age we share every up-skirt story. Kissing and books are everything to a boy at that age. I was drunk with anxiously still. When I wake up that morning. I could not wait till everyone had left and went about their way on that morning. The boobs were calling my name. Finally, the last goodbye was said and only Mike and Onna's range rover was left in the lot. I was sure I could get the magazine into my bedroom for the day. I just could not wait for them to leave, but when I went to the living room the down ladder was gone! Anxiously knotted in my belly and my heartbeat increased in my panic as I searched for this thing high and low. I just happened to open the basement door and looked down and there it was. Relief all at once replaced my panic. All I had to do was go down there bring it up really quick and get my magazine.

Mike an Onna rarely came upstairs and never really was ever home. Still our parents wanted us not to disturb them. That was my intension when I went downstairs. The aluminum ladder was flimsy enough for me to get it and go. I was going but that is when, I heard it, "Fuck me" my ears now heard the magazine calling out for me and I was coming. "Oh shit, yes fuck me" this time much more audible it was not the magazine calling it was Onna beautiful voice.

I put the ladder down and in the dimness of the basement corridor lights I listened to loud skin slapping and profanities that made the tent in my shorts come back. There room was all the way at the end of the hallway about 15-20 feet from where I was standing at the base of the stairs but as I crept towards Mike and Onna's room it felt like a mile long walk to get to it, but I got there, and my legs felt as I had walked a mile too. {Fuck me}" Onna screamed, and the loud smacks slaps kept on filling the air. My mouth felt dry as I brought my eye to the keyhole. There they were Mike behind Onna and on the bed. Onna on all fours held in place back and forth as he rammed into her from behind. I could not see it, but I knew he had his cock in her pussy just like the magazine read.

YES, YES do not stop fuck me fuck me Onna kept yelling looking over her shoulders as her tits and in gold necklace swung in tandem. "Perfect at one point I could have sworn she had spotted me through the keyhole and almost ran but couldn't. I thought we locked eyes. She stuck her tongue out like she could taste the sex. The more his heavy hand came down to smack her butt the more she screamed to be enjoying it all. Mike to me look like he was hurting Onna, but I know this was not pain and what I was watching was fucking. When I found my hand was making the "o" in my shock I had to detach myself from the keyhole. I crept back to the steps grabbed the ladder got the magazine went to my room and focused on making my cock jizz the new word for that day. Anxiety was not going to keep me up tonight. I looked at every page to see the multiple angle and positions to "fuck" in, and women liked to have jizz in their mouths. The one Mike and Onna were just doing was called "doggy style" according to the magazine. A really elegant looking white lady was bent over "enjoying the pulse of the black stallion shaft in her pussy while fucking her doggy style. Highly informative.

On that evening, I was to spent from the earlier activities of the day, that my mother even asked if I was sure, I would be ok to go to school soon. I assured her I would. The last day I watch Mike and Onna Fuck each other brains out again. I went for the magazine, jizzed a few times returned everything like the previous days, showered and like clockwork Onna would come in humming and bent into the fridge. As I imagined “doggy styling” her, she looked over her shoulder and caught me this time. I looked away quickly, but I knew she did. You want some? Her voice came from behind me. I could not believe it, but I had to answer right ‘umm” I started ‘it’s pretty moist’ she said, I turned to see her hold a large blueberry muffin. My racing little heart calmed. I smiled nervously “no thanks.” Till this day I think about fucking Onna, no offense Mike if you are reading this. (But that is when, where, who, what, and how I got my first hardcore lessons in sex-ed.)

As girl I will call Winnie was my first love or so I wanted it to be. She said I was her first but later I found out it was all wrong. No love, not her first and far from beautiful. She ended up fucking my friend and lied about that to but that is where I discovered revenge sex but that for another book.

Since then, I thought I have spent some time asking men and women questions about sex giving advice and sharing stories that we put together for your pleasure in this book. Blogs, email, text, and in bed tails of the wonderful tales of actual and fantasies of mine all completed about women from different walks of life. I have collected stories and panties to put this together for you. So, show some appreciation will you, and if you have got more of either let me know email me at 1alistmade@gmail.com.

I would love to really dig into it a little voyeur's club. It should be rather interesting as you read along the tantalizing tales will cause moisture ladies and throbbing fellas so be aware. Oh, and the kids may find it next to the gun at least they will opt for this rather then that right? Till this day I believe my dad knew I found the magazine and that Onna did see and tease me through the keyhole. I just may ask them by part two.

Christine N 44
New York, NY

Mr. Pain, I have just read one of your blogs and I must say you have got my attention. For starters, your eye for details is what keeps your stories sizzling from front to back (pun Intended) you seem to know a woman's body well is something I would like to find out on my own about.

I have been snooping around your profile and I think your fucking eatable fine dark slap of chocolate, just what a girl needs with a sweet look. Like a well one prime rib, I am eyeing you. I do not think you will mind if I am correct. I am real estate agent and I own a very popular piece of property here in Manhattan. I also see you have a serious fetish for high heels the come fuck me styles. I own a very wide variety of them that I am inviting you to review and rate as I fashion them for you. In return I will let you have me, as your personal submissive slut for the evening.

I have been waiting for an opportunity to get really fucked on these expensive surfacers but by an exclusive cock like yours, YOU GAME? For your services I will spare no expenses and suck you dry to pay off the debt I owe after your consultation of my sexy is complete. My pierced 36 dd's and tight pussy should serve you very well. BBC (Big Black Cock) titty fucked has been on my list for quite a while now. My clit is pierced too, so I am extra sensitive to touch even the friction of my panties that I wear anymore make me drip.

I read your response to my invite and finger bang myself at the office on a rainy day when I have got myself locked in. At home I have a rabbit and anal beads that keep me Cumming for hours. I hope your built to last like you say. I am thick woman but inactive far from the last lovers you have talked about in your blogs. I have a real apple bottom for a white woman. I often hear and I have always had it too.

Its time I get rated an a few things by a real pro. I just must be sure you know what I mean. I excel at everything that I do, and I aim to please all my clients and business partners. This will be no exception being the boss is fun. I am always usually in control and doing the rating not too many can survive me sexuality. But reading your books it got me thinking.

Pause now: this woman really spoke to me I have actually copied and pasted this from our emails of course had to go to the big apple and see what this woman really had to offer. I always go into these situations cautiously, always. Yes, it is because I have been catfished in public before and who has time for that.

We met at a comedy club in time square. She was just beautiful, tanned skin glossy lips and were glassed that made her look like a strict boss lady. Her wonderfully tight physic was much more stunning up close then the tits and dick pick we shared. They were nothing compared to the real thing.

I stood and went for a hug so I could get her big soft lurking tits push against me nice and early. At midway she kissed me I mean slightly tongue down my throat and groped my already excited appendage as she did so. I do not usually kiss on the first date. Who the fuck am I kidding I just do not do the public display thing. But she tastes like she smelled so I kissed her back nice and hard as I palmed her full even plumbed ass. We went as it at least 10 minutes before the server cleared his throat to ger our attention. We ignored him for at least two more minutes before breaking it off only to breath.

As I told him our orders Chrissy used her thumb to wipe my lips clean of her lip gloss and applied a fresh coat before she spoke. Tonight, we are going to dominate each other after in this city. Do you understand her tone was no nonsense and fucking turned me on to no end? All through the show she made sure my cock was incased in the o of her hand not even to give anyone a care even the Critics. Her phone started to ring. It must have been her rat of a husband; I thought as she took the call and excused herself from the table.

When she came back her energy seemed different, she sat across from me this time with her back to the show. Then I felt the tip of her pretty French manicured toes shaped in the black 6-inch stiletto heels slowly slide on my leg till it was between my legs. The server appeared at that I breathed a little relief, but then Chrissy looked away "excuse me take these back sir, we need them well done a little crisp on the edges "isn't that right daddy" she said knowing how salutary that sounded. I cleared my throat ignoring her toe probing my throbbing dick. "that's right mommy" we locked eyes, so she knew I was game.

I thrusted forward so she would rock back making her action noticeable to whoever was watching. Chrissy was a very naughty girl so that night when we got back to her condo, I made her keep every secret she had made with her many changes of shoes I fucked and spanked her like a savage in the wild relentlessly. I spared her no modesty for her challenges in public. Leaving my handprints all over her pale skin in bright red whelps made me cum so hard. I thought she spit some out when she took me into her mouth, as I yelled on your knees, I am Cumming, but she was fucking champ and drank my energy down in gulps. Even licking the tip and smacked my cock on her tongue to make sure there was nothing left to even wash off. Chrissy we will play again that is a promise.

I like quality things too and love exploring some new levels of erection with my "biggest fan" well that would be the only way to go about it. Right? I get hundreds of letters and emails that people desire for me to print but you are of the first ever and so vivid that I had to make sure you get into this novel. Thanks for your support and maybe not to ???? in the future. I could write about our next escapade in the next book that would be very much appreciated keep it coming ladies and gents.

Sex never gets boring it is up to us to keep it exotic and interesting. Stay safe but keep on fucking and getting fucked. I have gathered some not all the hottest stories and experiences written down for years. The ones that made my dick the hardest. Reality or fantasy it is amazing how we can design so many different ways to bust a nut. Chrissy, you have my word I will be in New York doing a book signing and if you are really game, we can hook up again. I still have your 1st business card. I will be hitting you up when my tour takes me there. All over again another juicy bite for sure.

Chrissy: Maybe I may have found a match a challenge worth my time. Being the submissive slave where, hungry for her master's big ass black dick is so up my alley. No one even me of being such a nympho do to how Strick and reclusive I tend to be. It is really all the bend up sexual frustration that I cannot seem to really get fucked out of me. Trust me I have tried. Those guys scare easy and just do not last.

Had a threesome with my old roommate and her man before they got married and that turned out to be boring, I fucked them both into submission and end up drinking champaign and using the bottle to get off while they slept. They so deserved each other. but you sure talk a mighty game. One only a pro could know. There is no guess about it, some aspects of orgasms your words alone make me cum. Come use me again!

My mouth and asshole will be more about my own greed. Only the best for the best so we will have whatever it is you drink. I read somewhere its tequila I get the best stuff on earth trust me. I will model a few fishnet body suites pups and skirt still I am sure I have got your full erection I mean attention, oops. Then you will fuck me till I have dripped dry. I want you to leave had prints on the pale skin of my ass face throat and tits. Do not you dare hold back. I will wear the shoes of your choosing a metal dog chocker around my neck, so when I am Cumming as you fuck me in my holes the chain cuts off my oxygen taking my orgasm to levels, I've only fantasized about. You walk me around on all fours fucking me out on my top floor balcony. The ground and stainless-steel surfaces. I am in the middle of my living room where the fireplace would be nice, but it is up to you.

Just keep that 12-inch cock of yours in my mouth gagging me as you yank on my leash to feed me dick. Slap it about my pretty face really hard. Take fist full of my red hair as I look up at you with that heavy veined dick to the back of my throat. I imagine you hog tie me and pour hot wax on my rose-colored nipples and clit, maybe you could speak some of that creole of yours? Oh, the voodoo you do. I have bought some whips I am afraid of that you can whip me raw with, and there is always my thick wet tongue and my even tighter exclusive asshole.

My long blond hair wrapped in your feet while I attempt to deep throat all that muscle or as you powered me like a runaway savage from the back, will be worth your while. Although I am white woman, 44 years old and spend 10 hours a week at the gym these days. My belly is tight my waist a 5 my ass seems to not be getting any smaller. As a bigger woman in fit my figure and was starting to get self-conscious about it till, I read your interest and realized, hey maybe I got it going on here. Thank you for that boast of confidence, we all need that in the world. I would cover it up as much as I could before then, I am certainly recognizing the head turns since my change in wardrobe. Still sophisticated and fashionable does not have to be boring or slutty ladies, trust me. Pain, I heard you like to suck toes. That may tickle but I would love to have my toes in your warm mouth while your dick is inside of me up to the hilt. I think I might scream just thinking about it, God!

Every evening on my train commute home I would break out your emails after a long day of work in the city and get a few sentences in before I got home by the time, I get to the front door I would need a shower and a new pair of panties. If I wore any that day. Of course, I get the built-up tension out using my shower head. Husbands by the woman you love a mobile shower head. Anyway, I take my run to the gym the whistles and howls keep me young I say. I pretend not to hear the guy's lude comments by wearing headphones that do not come on till I am in the gym. I am a New Yorker I need to keep aware of my surroundings, right? Its empowering to me to know that I am still sexy enough to distract in a city this big, you know. The run home is the most exciting to me. After I treat myself to an iced coffee, it is off to my condo. Once I am past the honking taxi drivers, the excuse me miss of the young men on Broadway, past my eager doorman and another round with my precious shower head.

Mr. Pain you should know I only use a towel to dry my hair. I like to air dry. I rarely am dressed in anything at all when I am indoors. A few well-placed mirrors allow me to keep an eye on my fitness progress. Laundry follows up calls, the news, social media while dinner is going yes, I do all naked. I am in bed with a glass of wine emersed in one of your videos or messages with the lights down low with my 10 mode 12” dildo I try to imagine me sucking your dick. Just bent over you with my heels so tits hanging and swinging as I bob and slurp that rock hard cock. You can just sit back and enjoy the show sir. Mommas get you.

Is it the arch of my feet my back or is it the elevation that gets you off in my stilettos Mr. Pain? By the time I have shifted into mode 4 I am near climax number two. Tell me would it make you cum harder to have a prude like me massaging your balls with your cock lodged in the back of my throat, could I take you over the top harder by looking into your eyes as I am gagging.

My steel gray eyes, and long lashes have been known to captivate. Well, I like to believe that is what has been getting me out of traffic tickets all these years. Or it may be that I always make sure the wells of my breast are peeking through my top. The light freckles make them even more promenaded climbing on top that dick riding you would be my pleasure starting slow till you have got me soaked and stretched enough for me to ride you like my favorite horse. It has been a while since I have really been fucked, I mean really fucked. I am really picky about who pets my kitty, shouldn't I be? I only ever get to mode 6 or 7 before I am dropping the remote or book and screaming and squirting all over the place. The 4th time I cum just breaks me into little time pieces I swear.

Let me ride your huge dick white it's in my pussy then switch to my ass I'm sure I'm not ready so you will have to force me to take it all in. Let me know when your cumming so I am on my hands and knees sucking your thick cream out of your shaft till my lips swell and my tongue is numb this time? me and gag me while you ??? me like there's no tomorrow, and once you've drained me of all my juices and you were paid in full with the last of your seeds on my face and tits. Please feel free to take a card and call me when your around or maybe looking for a home in the big apple or just want a bite or two of mine. Your biggest fan Christine.

ALEX: wow Christine, fuck yah I would love to come and be your consultant for another evening or two it would be my pleasure. I am so glad you understand that it would cost a great deal for me to travel and all that it takes to accommodate me. I would love to be your master in return. My heel fetish is true love. I do have a big heavy veined dick.

You are very well studied the subject that is Alex Pain a man can really appreciate that.

Jasmine H 29.
Morton MS

Alex let me start by saying your stories have really made me realize sex does not have to be so serious, safe, or quiet! I have dated males and females my whole life and always will. I love your details of the anatomy's. I found myself lost in a few of your stories. My neighbor and I have been licking and sticking each other all summer. I shared with her your stories reviews and the story about that naughty neighbor of yours from the earlier chapters. We both agree that it was hot. We have both also agreed that should the opportunity present itself we are going to fuck the shit out of you, hope you do not mind.

In detail we want to wear matching outfits like the other story only we will bring fruit and cream so we can eat it off you and you eat out of us. Lindsey's pussy is sweet enough I promise anyone she, would surlily cause a cavity. My light pussy stuffed with your monster black rod. She will ride your face in reverse cowgirl so we make out and be indulged in your nasty ways we think it would really be amazing. We want to switch positions the two of us till you have fucked and sucked us dry.

A black or Haitian guy with a big ass dick, that do not discriminate against white or Spanish girls like you, are really in luck. I am 5'7" 149 lbs. brown eyes, 32ddd's tits and a round ass. Lindsey is Cuban with platinum blond hair that compliments her golden blend with pouty lips, 30dd tits, a huge ass to beg for, her 130lbs 5'4 frame. We both are squirters I know how much you love that. I am a moaner she is a screamer. I just see her pretty green eyes now all lit up while you're gagging us with your pole. We both love it in the ass so we will be sure to meet every one of your desires at least twice over again.

We both so desire to be in one of your next books/stories. Follow us on social media, text me if your down. Trust me we will make it worth your time. I think we can be your best story yet. We are both country girls with plenty of energy. You think you have the stamina, our thick shapes will no doubt entice your Sultry words in your next book. Right now, Lindsay is in a black G-string and in a pair of pumps. I let her wear from my collection nothing else. Even as I am trying to send to you, she is kissing my neck with her soft lips. Our shower was one of those "You had to have been there" moments. She had her middle finger in my ass while lapping juices from my pussy. The powerful shower heads in my super-sized shower seems to intensify every second. I do not know how she is able to breath when I have her by her neck and one leg over her shoulder. I just love how her knees are like that. She makes me cum twice before I am on my knees with her bent over with my tongue and fingers pleasing her tight ass hole and cunt too. We will usually run out of hot water before all ideas that make each other cum are finished. I think it's the fact our boyfriends do not know, nor will we share this thing we have with either one. Sam my boyfriend he is ok, but I do not think I could trust him with all this ass Lindsey has. I have seen how he looks at her. Just the way Manny's Lindsey's man does me, my tits anyway.

We actually met in the wine and spirit store even though we have lived across from each other for 3 and ½ years before. Who could of guess the last bottle of Rose Wine during a pandemic would have led up to screams Squirts and storytelling. Fuck social distance. We both have been in the house anyway for quarantine while the guys work there "essential Jobs" in the city. When there around we might simply share a smile and little more, so the secret of the steamy shower is the last thing either one thinks we are meeting for.

Sitting in the house bored out of my mind made me venture over to the cute Cubans crib and offer to share the oversized bottle she had allowed me to walk away with at the store. Sure, we wandered what a woman's pussy would taste like. I think a lot of women wonder about this at some point in their lives. First time was in college watching my roommate walk around in her panties. She was delicious but just a girl like me. Lindsey is 33 and all women. After a few glasses of wine, we had shed our blouses to compare out tits. One thing led to another. I will give you details if you decide to write me into your next book and do some of those things, you are always writing about that make me squirm in my pajama bottoms when Sam decides to fall out early. My fingers have always done the trick and now, Lindsey's tongue is a great substitute. Her skin is so fucking soft I cannot resist. Point is I would like to have you in my bed I hope I am not being to frank no I really hope I am actually. Remember how you said we need not hold back nor be shy. So, there it is I hope to be approved for your magic ride. P.S. Lindsey wants you to know we are always going to be your biggest fans.

Alex: By now you've gotten my email approving you both for "the Mayle ride" I love your energy and confidence. You and Lindsey will have one hell of a story to tell too, I promise. Ladies' stamina I have got plenty and I Love all races of woman long as your curvy, clean, of ages 18 to 80, blind crippled and yes even crazy I am down to play. Your relationship status is not my business sorry fellas. Now, a few guys have hired me to romp with their ladies and it has been an honor and always will be.

You ladies have officially been entered in my top fans list, let Lindsey know that. We must make sure to make this one a hell of a story wont we. I really appreciate how on point your observations are to. Till we meet sexy. I want you to consider maybe a night out all three of us.

I think I would really enjoy showing you guys off. I keep imagining you and her breast spilling out the top of your bra's wide hips and wet lips. In high heels and flat stomach just flawless. I will want you two to loosen up so maybe take you out dancing at this exotic Spanish club I know. Of course, Tegula for me and I am going to guess a good bottle of Rose wine for you two. I am not really a dancer in fact I would much rather watch the two of you seduce each other. Whisper your kinky plans to each other. From my seat I will be eyeing you both like a predator. I want to watch Lindsey pull you close by your ass. I want you both to plant wet kisses on each other's necks and lips. Both of you watch me watch you. Your nipples will be nice and hard while you roam each other's bodies making my dick rock solid. The thought out you sucking my dick and licking up the sweetness your pussy's will be leaking will be on my mind as you two dance. I want you both to return and sit on opposite ends of me so I can reach between your legs up your skirt to feel your wet panties if you even decide to wear any at all.

Jasmine Since you seem like the one in charge whisper to me "We need your fucking dick in our mouths" After watching you two grind your pussies together on the dance floor I will be more than ready to oblige you. I want to feel the combination of your hands rubbing my cock through my jeans. I can't wait to watch you suck this big of a dick Jazz" Lindsey is going to say, like I am not even in the room. Once we get back in the limo heading back to your suite, I want her to put your hair in a messy bun while you unzip me and reach deep into my jeans to grab my dick by its head like a snake, before you go down to take it in your mouth. Lindsey pulls you up and slaps you. "May I suck his dick now?" You ask coyly with a horny smile and with a nod of her she guides you by the back of your neck down. Your warm mouth and tongue engulf me. Up and down slowly as you adjust your mouth and throat to my girthiness. Lindsey can let her huge tits out so I can suck her hard nipples all while she admires my size.

I want Lindsey to whisper in Spanish "how does that feel" while gripping the back of your head so I can fuck your pretty face. Lindsey can join you while you both gag and slurp on my dick. Taking turns going from the tip of my cock down my shaft to my balls. I want your tits swinging, I'm going to smack your asses to intensify yalls sucking and moans. "I told you we were gonna come for you" I want you to remind me when you come up for air. Jazmine your breasts look fucking awesome in those pictures you sent. I can't wait till you to let me tit fuck them while I suck the others clit between my lips. By the time we get to the room I would have made you both cum twice and spilled cum down both of your throats.

We will go into the shower so I can be an addition to the shower scene you speak about. I want to hoist you up on my shoulders with my face in your pussy pushing your fold aside with my tongue, as I dig deep inside you. Lindsey will be deep throating my dick while massaging my balls at the same time, I will keep switching you positions and places till the hot water runs out. Stamina for days I really got some dick control. I want to make your eyes roll back in the back of your heads. “Yessss Pop yess” I want to hear you scream and Lindsey in her Spanish accent as I turn up the tempo of my finger plunging in and out of your assholes.

Then while we are all still soaked and wet to the bed we go. I want you to lay on your back while Lindsey feast on that pretty pussy of yours. I will slide into her from the back and grab the back of her neck so moans directly into pussy.” Don’t stop” I want you to be taking both of us. I can’t wait to see her face covered in your juices when you squirt and switch spots. I want to fuck you in the ass for some reason it’s the way your ass sits so high. It just begs to have my heavy cock stretching it slowly till I am balls deep. I will hold you in place by your hips while I dick you down. Going from hole to hole till your dripping too. I want you to ride my dick while your neighbor rides my face and you two make out at the same dam time. Let’s go round after round till we can’t tell what’s sweat, water or cum. I am going to really enjoy you two if your down. My question is where is your man going to think you are while I am pulling your hair and pounding every hole you two have for a few hours? How about you guys stopped to vote, and the line was fucking crazy lol. I will see you two very soon.

Charles R. 39
Newport News, VA

As usual a woman walks past rolling her suitcase behind her. Thanks for loving me on as a stewardess one said as we waited for a cab on the sidewalk. Thank you love I smiled beneath the brim of my captain's hat. I am always calm, maybe a perk of the job that is captain of one of the biggest airplanes on the fleet. The pretty young lady walked past me "Have a good evening" I think she said. I was distracted by her tall slender figure, tight skirt, and the way her dark hair whirled around her shoulders. I have always been a sucker for details. I watched her get into the cab and as it pulled away from the curb, I could not help but remember what she and I had just done on the flight over LA.

First let me tell you I have got a beautiful wife at home, that I am very comfortable with. But I guess I always have kind of had a roaming eye. And my ego my Nancy says exalted my position with my company. In fact, it is probably why I am more often than not targeted by the attractive, sophisticated, and accomplished women. Especially the young flight attendants of the sorts. I LOVE Nancy yet still lust the rest. The attendants where usually from where we were flying to or flying from, beauties of all sorts. Although my wife is no idiot and in fact very much the opposite. She makes comments like “wash her off and get to bed. With a smirk that tells me she is not at all blind. But since her back surgery all Nancy is really able to do is suck my dick her and again. Even when I massage and suck on her big tits and eat her pussy like a starving street bum that finds pizza forgotten in a box “there’s only so much I can do” she apologizes after she cums soaking my mustache. She supports that a man does have needs so long as I always come home well that is how I have got it in my mind.

I let the young stewardess into the pilot’s cabin as I have promised the many of them before takeoff. Then some time midflight I sit her on my lap while the plane is on auto polit. Where I promise, I am going to teach her manors when we land. Yet sensitive these are very sophisticated machines. We are safe I promise you. To pour a few glasses of wine for only her and as usual letting my dick swell under there perfect asses. One evening, Mona who was from DC caught my eyes going over her figure. with a blush and coy smile, she warned me the flight was not long enough before boarding. Perhaps a career killing move but when the coast was clear I gave her a firm slap on the ass. Her butter soft 24-year-old ass felt amazing under her skirt. “Thank you, captain can I have another,” she whispered surprisingly without even looking back. As I adjusted the controls in the cockpit, I was thinking about throwing my cock in Mona’s openings. Then a soft knock was on the door. She uses the coded knock that would gain any employees access to the cockpit. She locked the door behind her pushed me back till only thing between us was the back of my co-pilots seat who was more than a great wing man. Tommy seemed to never notice. Maybe?

She put a finger to my hips stopping protest squatted down unzipped my pants and expertly pulled my dick over the elastic band of my briefs and kissed the tip of my dick very familiar move, but it got me rock solid her prep skills where good not like my nasty Nancy, but I guess the stranger's mouth is exciting enough. So, it always gets the job done. I have always avoided fucking in the cockpit I need space to really get off. Mona did not seem to be interested in my safety concerns or the co-pilots She bent over the empty seat pulled her skirt up panties to the side "fuck me now" she said barely looking over her shoulder. I entered her moist pussy I held her shoulder blades and rammed into her already slick twat for only about 15 minutes before I was ready to explode. Like Mrs. Nasty does in yalls many homemade Pornhub videos.
She hurried to her knees and sucked my cream down careful not to let not even the slightest drop escape. "Dam Baby" she whispered dabbing the corners of her lips clean with her painted fingernails. Looking up at me with her cute smile. I should get back she says before escaping into the cabin. The flight to DC was otherwise smooth.

Tonight, when I got home Nancy was asleep, her meds had been taking her down earlier every day. Dinners in the Microwave I love You" the note read on a cold beer in the fridge. I heard a buzz and discovered it was Nancy's cell phone on the charger. The contact saved under Mona had texted "mission complete- The Captain has landed. "Honey, bring a bottle of water" my wife yelled from upstairs as my heart pounded. I stripped down and threw my uniform in the dry-cleaning hamper, my briefs, and socks into the washer with the other soiled things waiting to be washed. I gave Nancy a long kiss before the bottle of water." I take it you had a good flight" I looked her in the eyes like when we had first met and told her I loved her before I went to the shower. Just before emailing this to, you I spent an hour making Nancy cum over and over. Tomorrow I am headed to Paris.

Alex: Hey Charly, Nancy got a sister?? My man you have struck gold no doubt about it. Keep her happy mand considering she is making sure you are. What is not to love there? Her being injured could have made her bitter, instead she is letting you get off. Under her control but still. I hope she gets better soon. When Nancy is better you could take her on a trip or two with you. Never tell her you know about the plants in case she decides to use others later after she is well. You will pass with flying colors, won't you? Anyway, let me know if you ever go to the middle east or Egypt, I hear the women of their lands are goddesses.

I could help but wonder if your co-pilot is part of her covert operation and he is there making sure all goes to plan for dear Nancy. And if so, what does she pay him with? Don't fuss now she's keeping your belly full and ball empty. Now if that's not how a woman keeps her man coming home, I don't know what is. There's nothing in the world like a selfless woman. Maybe you could return the favor when she's all better. She is obviously secure I hope you can be too. Yes, I can be booked for special events like this, just shoot me a line I got you captain. But meantime lick her like your last lolly you will ever lick.

My last girlfriend planted her girlfriend to catch me in the act only it didn't go as planned. Instead of reporting to my girl she herself started meeting me for rough sex and dick pix. I didn't know she was a plant till my ex showed me screen shots. Well, a few anyway of my deception. Even when it was over, I was still fucking them both like concubines with orders to please the king. Now that I think about it maybe they were just using me, huh? Well, isn't that just a bitch Had some smoking pussy, swallowed like champs, and took it up the ass. So, joke on you ladies can't pip a willing slut like myself. LMAO back to you my good friend you have found a goddess take care of her man… and oh you on your flights is it safe to say the attendants are for the most part mile high friendly? Just asking for a friend is all.

Well truth be told I don't have a mile high story yet but damn if I won't and soon. Closest I can even come to one is when I was 115 on a flight to Haiti out of Kennedy, New York. I was watching Jumanji on the small screen above. The cabin as a bit dim but there was enough light for me to catch some action from the side of my eyes where a couple that had to be in the mid-forties or early fifties just acted if no one else was there. The lady had her head in his lap just going up and down, he had his eyes closed and held her hair in a ponytail. She opened her eyes and caught me looking. I looked away of course but I looked over and she was still looking at making sure she took more of him into her mouth even through a smile with her mouth full. He must have came in her mouth she swallowed and gave me a wink

Tonya A, 31
Linden NJ Via email

My club just selected your blogs. Then I realized it was you. I do not know why I feel like one of your stories was going to be about me, but I wish you would ask me “Alex” lol. I am sure you remember me from high school or not, a lot happened since then. Anyway, I am just divorced, and I want to pick up your book and a 10-inch toy to keep my mind busy on lonely nights I know how nasty you are. The way you fucked me back then was ok I bet you are a lot better now. You have always had a big ass dick though I must give you that much. You really tore me up. Once I managed to get used to it, you where fucking well you know who. Till this day I think I can feel your cock in my belly, no joke.

I see your hair is much longer now. They are probably a great way to get you in nice and deep, huh? I would use it to help you find the spot to best position your face when eating my pussy. That used to be my favorite. The way you always tried to be gentle and so selfless with that pretty mouth of yours. Alex, you know it has been more than 10 years and still I have yet to been able to find a man or woman’s tongue whip me like you did. It is funny but even if I try to imagine it’s you with that nasty wet tongue of yours sucking my pussy, they just seem to be missing a few steps. You always made sure my pearl got the attention she needed before plunging your fat tongue into my holes. Just thinking about it makes me squirm in my seat.

I must admit I get jealous when I think about the women today you must be making crazy with that mighty mouth, you knew I needed to be soaked before you would try to stretch my tight little pussy. It used to hurt so good.

My heart used to pound out my chest as soon as you would start taking your soft lips to my neck and whisper the things you were ready to do to me before your really did them. These power huge arms of yours let you pick up my legs drape over your forearms as you pinned me against the wall to drive into me wet begging wetness. Dam I really miss that.

The rough kisses the way you help my tits in your mouth by my nipples as you plowed into me. Have the scratches I dug into your back healed completely? I hope I scared you. Sorry but not really sorry. I can't believe after all these years I can still feel you inside of me, feel your tongue in my private secret places, and how dare you invade my thoughts this morning. And the worst part is the more I type the more I remember things I do not think I really want to not remember right now. Is that crazy sounding to you?

My ex-husband found an old letter you wrote me in high school explaining how you wanted me to meet you at the old football field to suck your dick with a hall the way I did that time at my sister's party, remember that? Well anyway that was about a year and a half ago, maybe two, but he had never got it out of his mind. Even complained that I never tried that trick with him. "I was sixteen" I tried to explain to him, but he would not let it go. I mean I did not think to do something like that to my husband at the time and maybe I should have stolen a trick from the past for him. Then again, I did not think I would appreciate him bringing some gimmick he used on his past whores and sluts, make sense?

But this mother fucker brought this up so many times I thought he would one day find you and shoot you, he is a state trooper by the way. So, one day I just went to pick up a pack of halls the winter blue just like you taught me. I cooked him a hot meal and we showered and as we make love, I broke out the cough drop on him. Would you believe he got angry about it and started this big argument who gets mad with their dick in a woman's hand and about to get throated you know how I do. Long story short we ended up not speaking a few days but while doing his laundry I found a hall wrapper apparently it was cool for Nikki the waitress to steal our trick. Thanks Alex and fuck you for that!!!! You probably will not put this one in your next book, but I thought you should know anyway by the way if your ever in town swing bye, same address. Bring a few winter blues, will you??? TTYL
PS. I am a BIG girl now!!!

Alex: Did not even know you were married, or I would have showed up drunk. Tonya I was better than fucking "OK" first bitch. LOL now, how are you? First, I will not admit nor deny I will use any of our escapades in any of my books all names till now have been changed for protection and respect understand? I do miss that fat ass of yours and my god your tits where fucking perfect in high school. And what is this married thing, why no invite, DAM! Probably for the best tho I would have probably fucked you somehow and made you reconsider locking down. Shit, that may have saved you money and todays heartache too. I am glad you are into my writings still. Enjoy your toy I have a few friends with great deals on that stuff. Quick question you sucking dick better? Also,

Thanks for the invite next time I am out that way a quicky could not hurt, or could it? Let us find out shall we love?

And if you're still reading this novel let's face it, we got you turned on, open and you can't get enough of pain. A glutton for pain you can say. In private all alone, with friends or group or can't with just your lover, the steamy words of the novel really work to have you Cumming back for more, isn't that right. And if this is your 1st ALEX PAIN contact. Well, you are in story for a ride or a few. To my readers and contributors that have submitted your love life's issues concerns opinions and raunchy story with me to create this collection Thank You. Keep it hot and naughty out there.

As you'll read this my fans, friends haters crushes, exes even next exes have all found a way to contributes to this their views, imagination opinions, dream nightmare, fantasies, and remarks so much I had together them up and create thinks enticing read for you. Please keep it Cumming, I love to read your thought no matter how dirty, strange or ummm different they may be all are welcome to skeet on my sheets. That is right squirters welcome.

Miyah 26,
New Haven CT

I have discovered life is too short to not explore the vast wonders. So, out with the old in with the new. "New Year new me". My new boyfriend is sexy as fuck, smart and has plenty of money. He is 6'3 Mexican and black body of God and respects me unlike my ex-boyfriend Mike. Ralphy is an amazing thing is he is 22 and to save his life he just cannot eat my puzzy the way I like. At first, he told me he did not do it at all, but I was not going to let him get away with that. I give good head, so I want good head in return. Mike the bastered, he is a lot more experienced I guess that comes with age and had the most amazing mouth I have ever had. I just did not have to ask he would wake me up in the middle of the night by sucking my clit something serious even if I had kicked him out for another one of his lies.

Ralphy has a bigger dick then the 36-year-old Mike, but even with that I feel like he is really shy or unexperienced with it. For example, he is way too rough before I am even wet and not aggressive enough when it is all I really need after a hard day at the office, just a really nasty hard screw to get me off relieving my frustrations. So, I have been thinking of letting Mike do the deed at least since he has been begging to anyway shit, he owes me that much for being such a fucking scum bag, right? Alex what should I do here? I am too young to be having a bad or and desperate sex. I am 5'5 130 lbs. I am in great shape hazel eye Carmel skin and fun. I really would appreciate any suggestions you might have for me.

Alex: Miyah you sound really sexy send me a picture, but anyway your absolutely right. You are too young for these complaints in the bedroom, and I am about to get some hate mail for this but to hell with Mike, he did not treat you good enough to be getting good pussy and head still. Sorry Mike you fucked up. Now for Ralphy he is young, and I keep hearing the new generations "Don't eat Pussy" SMFH! If he is good guy young or not, I think you should be patient and teach him what you are into.

I watched pain with my younger girlfriend till she was eat my dick like Sarah J and Briney Bea. When they are young there is lots of room to improve. Text him links to the videos you like open up the conversations more before you go play around on him, you never know he might turn into a hell of a love maker after all. Lubes and x-tube is your answer to great honest orgasms. Thank me later with concert ticket, porn, good wine or your phone number or something. Look its human nature to smell fire and run. But thank God we have those individuals that actually run toward it to and eliminate that danger. Mike will never stop doing whatever he did to you to others if you are not showing him what he has lost because of his nature. Now if that twat is as good as you claim it to be you need to be easy on just distributing it out to whoever whenever it will lose it powers otherwise. Wear and tear show up on anything under the heavens, please do not end up wall-less.

Miyah from around the way" Once a man eats it up, he is going to want to beat it up and in the heat of the moment it will more likely than not happen. Freaks like us have a lot of sex. Thing is a man will not stretch out or lose the elasticity that keeps that pretty box of yours tight and juicy.

I recently went to a bike club in Philadelphia to have a few drinks with a bunch of my friends. Wyde body is the place to be on any given weekend. As the night went a few hundred or so woman cycled in and out. Then in walks a super sex bomb shell. 5'5 light brown eyes, her thick legs were shown up due to her noticeably short skirt, her smile was at a devious in a sexy way. I took the first chance I could offer to get her a drink and sure enough she was down for a few shots. It did not take too long before we were both shit faced and stumble into the back seat of my truck. Her halter top came right off. I dove for her plumped melons. She smelled wonderful even the slight sweat that was between us, was pleasantly intoxicating.

I slipped two fingers into her midst entry body I guess she must have forgotten to wear panties. Her moans filled the steam air as I went back and forth from one brown nipple to another all while thrusting fingers into and out of her pussy till, I was certain she was ready. She was practically leaking like an old pipe. "This is going to be some good ass" I was thinking. She was pressed against the back passenger window while submitting to me attacking on her. “Let me suck that dick poppy” she said. I was not going to argue with that one bit. I sat back and she positioned herself on all fours on the back seat got my dick out and went to work. Back seat professional.

I kept pleasing her by pumping my hardness into her warm mouth and my fingers into her dripping folds, smacking her plumped booty to encourage her to keep up the good work and she obliged willingly. The sight of her feet cross while incased in her red heels, like she was concentrating on a very serious task, really made go for the gold. “Hey, you get on top” I whispered in her ear. “Uh-um she responded with my 12 inches lodged in her throat. She was slurping spiting gagging and slapping on my rod just the way I like. She must have realized after thirty minutes of fucking her face I was not going to cum like this.

Finally, she came and decided she would return the favor by getting on top. Soon as I was in, I sighed in disappointment. She still pretended to be tight by sliding down slow. No grip I mean at all. Felt like I was humping the air in an empty subway. I took her by the throat and kept slamming her up and down on my cock making her tits bounce hard. “Maybe I will cum up the face? Nope nothing. I faked one sobered quick lay “waste of time and tegula” so please Miyah do not burn up that pussy by putting to many foreign objects in it. Talk to you soon.

Belinda s 47
Lincoln, NB

About a month ago I met a younger man in his early 20's on the social media site. I am shy and new to the whole thing. I think the hardest part for me was to decide what picture I should post. I am trying to make a good impression all while trying to be irresistible at my age. Then making sure none of my family friends, or co-workers ever spotted me on there, like so many themselves had been caught in very compromising positions and had to do some explaining.

I been told my cleavage is ok, they are enough to grab the guy's attention. It has been a power move for me my whole life anyway so why not right. "Hey if you have got it flaunt it" I say. It does not last long anyway. Once I start clicking on this, I then figured out the privacy settings and how to block individuals I did not want to access to my page. I was actually surprised to see so many people from my community on there considering it is a dating site. I bet they wish they did what I did to safeguard myself on this site, but then again maybe it was their intention to be seen. Even Lee my neighbor with the big ass dick that I have been watching through our window since I moved here 5 years ago.

My husband well ex-husband now only wish he had a dick like that. He might have killed me if he ever caught me checking Lee out. When I saw him on the site, I almost requested him as a friend, but I just did not want the thought of him just coming over for anything more then to fuck me senseless with that ridiculously huge cock of his. He really is fucking pig headed son of a bitch who has women of all ages, races, and time of night going in and out of his house since Kelly his ex-wife left him for the Mexican guy Manny that use to work for Lee. Go figure, right?

Well anyway I made sure to block him so he wouldn't be all in my business. People these days have their noses in everything. The world would be a much better place with people they are just always into another person life all the dam time. It was about 2 hours into it before I was done getting my sexiest pix posted. I am heavier woman these days compared to my earlier ones. So, I find myself a bit more self-conscious. my sons' friends though seem to like it. I am sure it's probably embarrassing to him but very reassuring to me. The way their eyes seem to go to my belly and arms. Youngers lick their lips the geezers purse theirs. That the main reason I figured I try this one out on the web site my ex-husband had landed his mistress on. Shit what is good for the gander has got to be good for the goose.

Took me a little while to figure it all out but when I did, I see why so many people spend so much time on those things. We have been texting directly Darrick and I. Turns out he is a barber and with my night schedule we never really speak on the phone texting or sexting has been our thing. I even found my self-trading nudes with this guy. He loves my body as is, he says and his is 6'5 dark skinned six pack having ass does not need to change a thing. At my age being impressed is a rare, but this boy keeps making that moment over and over. It's something about his smile and confidence that makes the moistness between my legs heavy. I am still very active being a tour guide in my city keeps me on the move. I have promised to hold him in place with my legs if his strokes are as long and powerful as he likes to claim. He tells me he is going to bend me over and "beat that pussy up" I have still been waiting for the right time to see if he can walk the walk to back her talk. At this point I don't know if it's my own issues keeping us from linking up for a ramp in the streets or scheduling. But I am going to fuck this boy till I have no more fucks left and he better fuck my brains out the way he keeps promising. I might even suck his dick and balls if he is everything, he says he is.

The whole no condom thing could be what it is for me too. I am too old to be knocked up by anyone and his young ass probably laying around with all kinds of girls. Can never be too careful I say. It has been a long 2 years since I had some dick, 7 years since I had some good dick, but I am still not in any rush to have anything go wrong trying to please anyone, anyone including myself. I know where the errors lie, and I dare not fall into any obvious errors.

Alex: When you know better you do better" have fun but be safe it is a key thing. Physically and mentally, I am a cougar lover myself. I know the experience you bring to the table is really what it is all about for us. The no strings thing sometimes is hard to define if we are making too much contact (more often a week) mainly because it is so good the emotional and or physical. Getting my dick sucked by a woman that has more than enough practice is mind blowing. The control she takes when she is determined to cum is a whole world in itself.

Tip to my younger readers age brings about understanding of oneself. Know exactly what we want with maturity as far as sex goes and just how to get there. I want to cum for sure but not before I am making her cum. The young ladies that have had the privilege to be handled by me in the bed or car, whatever will be to my determination to make them submit to a screaming orgasm. In fact, that's what makes me cum. their satisfaction. Older women will say I had to be made calm with verbal commands and shifted like a 5 speed to get me to where they wanted. Some like it rough their asses slapped and fucked. But most want to enjoy it at their slower, smooth pace. I am always willing to learn.

Belinda, keep training him to be what you like he will do as you please. Anticipation to be having more sex than ever before. Younger man has time and enjoy that can potentially be controlled with some training but don't keep him waiting too long, and a youngster has a low attention span and get bored easily when not stimulated. He may very well just move on. Get it while it's hot Belinda! Thanks for sharing

Moly T 37
New Windsor, NY

Alex I am 5'7" brown eyes, short dread locks, brown skin, pouty plump lips, a small waist, large ass, 28 tits, and I am Jamaican and English mix. I am an IT for a large company in New York. I hope I am going to fit in your nasty yet classy class of woman. I have read enough of your material to know that's the kind you like. I am 140 pounds all curves. My twin could be Ashley Graham people say all the time but she's a little taller, I think. You have compelled me to finally write down my nasty, stepping out of my class for just a moment, just for you handsome.

I date here and again, just haven't found anything to serious or special enough to lock it in with. My family and friends think it's because I am too focused on my career to find "A Good Man" if there's such a thing. No offense. In reality, I just need more then I have been able to find with the ones I have been with. For example, love big brain but I need a big dick too, not often together. I need a man that's going to lay back and be patient enough to let me tease him with a dance in my sexy outfits and heels I like it rough but start slow, I want to be teased before debossed. The guys I find are very eager then premature on top of it all. Long sessions of sex are what I need the quickies they offer are fun when I'm in a rush, but that's not often. Lick my ass suck my toes, and please do take your time eating my pussy fellas.

I believe I am professional decency, but I dated a guy that happened to work for a company that I had been assigned too. Of course, appropriate time for quickly I am thinking of texting to him. He comes out as I am working at a woman's desk. I did not know if it was making him nervous that I asked him to meet me in his office, so I could "suck that big black dick" of his or if it was my surprising him in general. Then I saw him looking on the desk I followed his line of sight and at first, I did not see it. Just before I could say anything the woman's whose desk, I was at came back. Hi baby I just came from your office to see if we could dip out early for lunch since the systems down and our lovely IT team is in "I was a little shocked at first that Mr. Pine had a Mrs. Pine at home, the desk name tag confirmed that much. "I will be a while you guys go ahead and take your time" I said with a wink and a condescending tone I was not in control of at that moment. He only nodded and hurried out of there. I giggled to myself because my pussy still got wetter than ever thinking I could and probably would have him when I wanted. He was getting boring till that happened.

Two more months than I cut him off. I don't really expect anything from most guys, but I would like to be able to secure myself a good fuck that's selfless and sexy. I read your last blog, you're a freak. I have come to the conclusions that we should definitely hook up here and again. You can certainly "eat and beat" my pussy up any day Alex. I am sure that we are compatible enough to really get something nasty still classy going on between us.

Email me back let me know what you think of the pic I sent you to your personal email. 1alistmade@gmail.com right? And if there's anything there to explore between us. Hope to hear from you soon "Mr. Nasty too."

Alex: Molly, molly, molly, you really do sound classy and nasty enough. The pix you sent are hot as fuck, I am heart eyes emoji. I am seriously wondering how a woman as fine as your self hasn't found a man willing to do it all. Mind right, money right, body tight checking every department so far. Bad and bougee huh? I understand your allowed to seek out only the best in life and in bed too. I would love to get ahold of you and create a new story, no doubt about it.

I am thinking about doing a New York book signing soon, be there to get my hotel room key, go and get dressed in that lace and heels your speaking of. I would love to watch you dance, my tongue will touch your everything before it plunges into your wet folds from every and any angle you desire. Round after round I will see if I can't become a frequent flyer. I have been known to be too much but that sounds like what will be just enough for you. So, lets link up and find out how many licks it takes to get to our centers. Till then Molly oh and tell Mr. Pine I said way to fumble the ball was his wife hot at all?

Summer L 40
Baton Rouge LA

I met my fiancé August 2017 gave him back the ring in December 2018. Nick was a very cool guy, but he lost his well-paying job for using a racial tone at a meeting. Then he stayed home played games ordered sports matches, that I had to pay for. Together we could afford anything but now we had to sacrifice some things, but he could not realize it and I could have been ok with that, but on top of all that he just one day went dick dead on me. It made me feel so unwanted.

Long story short we went our separate ways. I have been taking time for exploring my hidden desires. My fantasies are wild and maybe unusual. I get to tell it full detail. Nick really had no idea what he was dealing with. I want to be walked around a lush home with a on leash and fucked randomly by a big fat long dick. I want to be slapped, raped by a man breaking into my house while I am doing laundry, and plugs, beads have always interested me. I want to get caught sucking a big black man's dick even though they intimidate me that fear is sexy none the less. I like a bunch of guys from my local bar to trap me inside so they all fuckd my holes on the pool table. I want them to really abuse and use me, spitting on me pouring their cold beers on my tits while fucking my pussy and asshole. I want to be fucked like a slut called a slut and whereby a team of handsome well-endowed man of all races. My mind can go on with this shit forever.

I am only 165 lbs. I wear glasses, small A cup tits, only 5’6 and often overlooked for the fuller figured woman around me, but I know I have got the nasty that many men crave. Nick could have learned this if he worked at communication. I mean dam, he did not work he should have had all the energy and talk in the world for his “soon to be” right? I hope Mr. Right comes along to make me cum and is not intimidated by my sexual appetites. I am proof big things come in small packages.

I want to slide down on a hard dick totally uninhibited and bone it till he grabs my ass to hold me in place till he fills me up with his hot cum. I want to jump off and suck him dry the way Cardi-B talks about in that song. Every woman I believe has a really wild side. I loved being looked at by men when I am out from behind. I know they are thinking about how, but they would like to bend me over and savagery fuck me. The thought of that make my panties really wet. Don’t get me wrong my live-in man could be all the above if he ever decided to.

I am getting into the spontaneous maybe even dangerous mind set lately. I used to think it was all about being pretty but even my ugliest friends are always having really raunchy sex in every place imaginable. I refuse to be held back by Nicks boring ways when it comes my freedom. This is not the middle east where some thought and action are frowned upon in a moral standpoint, not saying I don’t respect it. But we are not there yet, so I want nipple clamps and spankings please. And to be honest the more he is against other races the more I want to have one inside me. The whole racist thing just is not for me.

Rodney from my study class make remarks about "Fucking snow bunnies" and to tell you the truth it turns me on. The fact that he does not care what race a person is and keenly aware that good pussy comes in all shades. Ecstasy does not have a color and I am really sure of that fact. Besides all that crap I need a real man that is not afraid of other people and certainly not afraid to treat this pussy like his playground and his personal buffet. I just think I am too young to be limited to one mondain kind of pleasure. I am a young goddess, nerd excitement, explosion, and earth-shattering orgasm while I still can. Nick must understand change is good to keep me.

To think I almost asked him to have a threesome with my friend from work Chenell a black vixen. She my black barbie, I swear she has a body like one of those girls from the videos. She happens to love white man and women. With Nicks grumpy ass fired for being a fucking dick the last thing I am going to do is bring him some of that home. He would probably embarrass me anyway with his weak ass redirect concerning race. I am going to find me a BBC soon enough and I just might take pictures for Nick is that too much? Either way I am going to live life that's for sure. Alex, am I wrong for feeling like this be honest?

Alex: Yes, you are love! First, I don't know why black men scare you. We are no different than any other men in most ways. Matter of fact we are really into white and other race women more then you know don't let others negative views effect the connection opportunities boo. Aside from that love your cravings their sexy and if you can find a guy or two that you can open up to you will be having a lot of fun. Nick should have done more inquiring by maybe a tip here and again may have helped. You probably have a pretty little pussy too, not too many guys wouldn't try you out. I have fucked smaller women with high stamina, and I love the many positions your bodies can go into. My foot on the back of your head while I long stroke and spank your ass is my favorite. Summer, you would make a man's winter really hot. Mr. Right might be a lot closer than you know, put out a little bit more to find your match.

Ebony t 29
Dover, DE

What is up Alex I have always wanted to get up close and personal with you this opportunity is amazing though and gives me a chance to say things that I might not be allowed to say or might even be frowned upon. If I said them aloud. So, thanks daddy! Lol Clearing my throat. Listen fellas I am going to tell you that I am a highly successful, proud black woman. I have a child and my own everything. Thing is, the man I wanted is far gone, so at this point I am "living my best life" I am really built like a chocolate Monroe 5'5 26 B 6" waist round ass. My flawless complexion and teeth. I have been hunter for a while not of wild beast in fact very tamed ones. Yes, I am speaking of husbands, ladies I am sorry but if your husband is fine and paid, I will get him. Not to hurt you or hate on you it is because he will have to go home make sense?

I like to get my rocks off I will even suck his dick for you ladies who still fail to realize he will risk it all to get sucked off especially by a pro mouth like mine. I spend a little of his cash on bills and thrills and off he goes. I do not want a man of my own, I just want to borrow yours. I will not fight about them you all, me I will be for him if he has a fat dick and fatter accounts. So do not bother for real. I thought I was the only hunter for a while, but I am not. Many of us are young, the older men's weakness. We look for wedding rings and confidence. We meet up in packs all over and go over the list of the who's who and who's nots.

One of our huntresses lives near you and tells fiery stories of you spending time with pretty lady and a baby boy. I keep things like that at the back of my mind. And in case you are wondering I can love, just don't need to. I am infatuated with one man that I can't have, so I guess wild sex and hash money will have to suffice. I don't know exactly what you think of my breed, but I can assure you we have been around for a long while and not going anywhere anytime soon. In fact, our sorority just keeps getting bigger and better. You beware, we are everywhere and on the prowl. Shit we are everywhere you are looking for fellas. Next your wife's nudges, pokes or smacks you cause your attention is land on our firm asses, bellies, legs, and lips. Know you're in the presents of a huntress and if your wallet and balls are hard. We will gladly empty them both. We aim to please Just keep that in mind.

A little research and we will identify their net worth and cock size. Most men will just come along, because wives really think they don't have to try anymore once they have got the ring. Or that he doesn't know about her little dirty secrets he found snooping or told by her "best friends" who is also a hunter. I don't hate wives just love their selfless husbands. I let them Fuck me in the ass, mouth, the car, the bar, his friend's house, your beds and anywhere else he desires. I have even double teamed them with my fellow huntress.

Never am I going to love your man girl so don't worry I will cut them off if he even tries to say those words to me, don't worry about it. Call me the side bitch if that makes you feel better, but I get the money up front that's all that matters to me. My lifestyle is a tad irregular, buts its exciting and profitable. Don't call me a whore, they fuck for free, a ho is more like it. My girlfriend Erin is the blond hair green eyed version of me in case you're thinking my man only likes white girls lol. We come in all shape sizes and colors. Guard your hubbies cause its always hunting season. "It isn't safe" by default. By the way Alex is there a Mrs. Pain? Inquiring minds would really like to know?

Alex: Ebony I really am conflicted on how to answer to this one. I mean on one end I understand and fancy the whole catch and release thing. I mean just looking up for a good fuck and suck session here and again isn't anything to frown on. I mean many of us do. When the one doesn't want to be you shouldn't just lay down and die. Shit life is short but fun. Get that pretty face and pussy fucked as much as you can before you wake up one day and realize you can't at your age, and if my imagination of your body is on point, fucking is going to be a sport your great at right now. Best part is you can get even better.

I like the whole "huntress" idea. You said, have been spotted by one of your pack, huh? Now I am wondering who it could be. And where she sees me with "PYT" (pretty young thing). Those reading waiting to read the lines into deep personals, keep reading. I will give a little here and there. But back to miss Ebony miss snatch your man. Are you keeping tabs on me?

Now on the other end of this, all of you point out some of the ladies may be upset with you forgetting about their husbands. That is a very serious worry you may want to tread carefully around. I have known some very vicious ladies in my day that will fuck you up about their man's dick in your mouth, physically or metaphorically.

You ~~A~~are all probably the most hated if other women know. You're a "huntresses", am, I right? I sure you're getting plenty of play too. There's plenty of husbands out their board with that wife that won't try new things. The wife that doesn't suck a dick or at least learning should not even have gotten a second date ~~never the less~~nevertheless a ring and a last name. fuck that? Plus, you have those guys that are sex addicts' "players" with cash to burn.

I have a friend that just had to see if he still had ~~to see if he still had to see if still had~~ it, plus his wife is a true fucking nag. I actually recommended that he fuck his slutty porn star looking neighbor. Just to get it out his system and save his marriage and the expensive break up. That's called "using your head". Ebony, look a nasty girl like any red blood new in the world. I just hope you're being safe and not exposing your daughter to the fuck shit you do. Take what you're doing serious if it is your sport and do not, repeat do NOT tease or throw what you do in either women's faces. That's what could make shit wild and dangerous. Take my advice on that love.

In closing, go to say not all husbands can be got some wives care just so fucking awesome their men can't wait to get home to them. So, while you may be aggressively seeking and recking homes of those who have moments of weakness for a pretty face and body, last issues and those who just can't seem to get their wives to be as nasty as Nancy. There still is a great bunch of good healthy relationships out there. I personally if and only if I was claiming to be in a relationship with anyone. She would be down with us bringing home a nympho here and again, no time to be a creep. It isn't fun if the hommie isn't getting none. My lady has to be my hommie, a comrade of mine before she got a ring outta of me. Whoever it is that you are in love with may see or know about the shit you do, men talk too much and maybe the reason he keeps you away. You ever consider not being huntress. I am not hating or loving in fact extremely interested in your lifestyle. I just have to put these thoughts into context for our readers.

As I say often "Live life to the fullest" just try to be the best at what you do avoid doing anything you will regret in the future. And please keep an eye out for the

"Huntress slayers "I am telling you, there are really out their snooping around and might show up at our door step my love.

Morris 43
Elint MI

So recently I was going thru my old things, and I found an old phone my ex=wife had. I powered it up and surprisingly it didn't have a password on it. Call it what you want but I started to go thru it before resetting it. Of course, the bitch has text from a bunch of different guys even her email seemed to be her little hiding spot. I go in her photo album and find light dicks dark dicks and even shots of her pussy she sent out. "Fucking Whore" I say out loud like she was in the room.

I was going through this phone for an hour discovering the truths of this woman I thought I knew. Then I find the video album!!!! Where she's got herself bent over the phone, her tits out as a faceless man with a baritone voice and black powerful hands is drilling in her from the back as she moans, hisses and screams "Shit fuck my tight little asshole fuck yeah" I feel my whole body ready to blow. I just wanted to kill her and who ever this mother fucker is drilling deep in my wife's ass. Worst part has got to be the whole eleven years we had been married she would not let us do shit like that asking, "what kind of girl, you to be me for" "Its unholy" and all types of bullshit. Slut seemed to be doing all sorts and kinds of "unholy" shit the whole time.

My brother said I should post it on social media but as a moderator I know it wouldn't go far. Still, I text and emailed a few to a few of her contacts. It made me feel a little better, but the part of this that I am having issues with is that now I am over it I am enjoying her getting fucked by other men. Videos she sent of her playing with her pussy. Even one where her former boss is nailing her right on his conference desk. Alex man I am losing it. I mean I am watching man after man fuck her in every position under the sun and her deep throat these guys time and time again. My new black hotter girlfriend does not know I have been fucking her with these images in my head the whole time. Why can't I shake it? I mean I think I like porn as much as any other man in the world. But the excitement is profoundly different when watching my very own wife being pounded like a cheap whore.

I guess the best way for me to explain it is rage meets restricted lust. Her body is ok, but it is something about her being taken by another man that heightens my fierce desire. My limitation drives me crazy like a man that may be in dire need of water that he can see and smell it in the distance, it is just unreal the wanting that is so inviting. I caught a group of guys watching my girlfriend getting stuff from her trunk when she got back from the gym on Saturday morning part of one wanted to go out there and grab her by the ass and give her a long kiss before helping her inside the house. Showing the young punks, she was taken, and her owner was close. But there was a part of me that fantasized about letting them help her with her things. Then convincing her that I was gone long enough for her to give them a blow job and some of that tight young pussy. While I watched from the living room closet with my dick in hand. Yes, I know that sounds crazy and I didn't even know that it was a thing the day I had discovered it in my ex-wives phone. Then I went online and found that the category of my fetish fell under the fuck my wife searches a pretty loaded list top.

These boys play victim while these women get raped by a bunch of guys as he is made to watch in humiliation. I don't think I am the only man experiencing this kind this. Do you think it is a disorder or weird? I just had to talk out loud Alex.

Alex: well, that's not the worst I have heard Morris, Voyeurs and swinger do this. I think if you had found a way to communicate better with her then or your girl now you could have kept your marriage and experience a very interesting lifestyle. Maybe if she doesn't kill or sue you for passing out the images you could still have a chance. Then again you could have just advertised her to the next Mr. Right. Just saying and it's all in the approach when it comes to "Ass fucking" be nice and gentle. Some women are self-conscious and some plain afraid of the pain. Comfort and timing my good sir. Comfort and timing make if feel good and she will be begging for it.

Another thing I want you to remember never go through a Partners things if you're not married. If your married it is a little different cause you have made a serious commitment. The vows you took make you, one where there should be no secrets no matter how dirty. It should be shared and explained, so she gets a bad mark in my book for the other life she was living. That life you may have even been ok with it seems. Only if there was better communication and some dam honestly at home. Sure, you told me your side but, I would really like to hear hers something is missing here. I am not calling you a liar maybe it is just a longer story cut short for the purposes of getting to the point. So, if you're the ex-wife reading this, I would like to hear what you have got to say.

P.S. the bad mark for being a sneak and married stays in case you're wondering, but if you're not married or become unmarried do not and I repeat do not search your partners things to find out what they are doing on the side. Your feelings 90% of the time will be hurt.

If you lack communication or emotional checks, people hide things from you. When you first start fucking it is the best time to tell your mate all the freaky little things about you if they run off cool, if not then you might be on to something. No one wants to be known as the whore sure I get it but if that is what you really are be proud of it shit. I love sluts and whores as long as they are honest and don't mind me exploiting it a little in my books and videos that way, we both enjoy our lifestyle. You are a cock hold Morris they are voyeurs looking in on their very own lovers and that's cool.

I had a very good-looking couple approach me when I went to a resort In the Poconos in Pennsylvania. The woman at least 45 years old was super fucking hot bleached blond hair maybe c cup tits and a voluptuous ass and went well with her wide hips. I loved how well she seemed to keep herself groomed that really turned me on. Manicured hand, pretty feet in her wedged sandals. Her legs and the rest of her where shiny, freckles, and well-tanned. Even her makeup was light in application but still made her natural beauty pop.

I ordered a tequila and ginger ale on the rocks when I caught this attractive woman looking deep into me while her man or whoever he was leaning into her as she sat on the stool two away from mine. She ran her finger through the man's hair and whispered into his ears all while peering over his shoulder into my soul. You can just feel a person staring I think you know that feeling right? Anyway, I looked away and back when Greenday the music playing paused for a few seconds before the feeling came back. I happened to catch a movement in her leg she was parting them so her explorer could thrust deeper into her glistening shaved pussy. I almost chocked on the cool whip I had just let into my mouth I have loved "Green Days" music since by the way. Even when she noticed I noticed she only looked at me deeper biting her light pink colored lips. When her man turned and caught me looking, I thought I would have an issue.

He was about 6 feet 135 average build, white guy very cool a bit long and jet-black hair styled backwards. She looked away pulled her skirt down and went to her now watered-down drink as he made his way to where I was sitting. I outweigh this guy by a hundred pounds, but his stride was confident, so I got ready for confrontation by standing up. His stern expression turned to smile when he was only 5 steps out of my personal space. Then he said. Like the doe reaching out with the very hand that was just has the pretty dame ready to blow. I shook it anyway to make sure I could control his next move. The fingers felt cold, and damp and I think he wanted me to feel that "I'll have what he is" then like John Doe said to the bartender as he took the stool next to me.

I watched his calm demeanor and realized he wasn't her to fight. I sat down and kept an eye on him. So, I know you may think I am off my rocker coming out of that over there, thumbing over his shoulder and coming over here to talk to "Shawn" I liked swiftly." you Mr. Shawn but Jane "like Jane Doe" wanted me to ask you join us this evening, no I am not gay no offense if you are. But she has this fantasy I want her to have it before we tie the knot. This as he began scribbling on a napkin is our cabin number I am thinking after dinner around nine will be perfect. If you don't show I will understand. If you, do you will never regret it man, and we would really appreciate this. John didn't even let me respond. Just left a hundred-dollar bill and the fresh drink and went back to Jane who on cue stood got her clutch purse and hooking Johns' arm and walked past me still staring the light out of the bright warm day.

At first, I figured this was some kind of joke or dare he had to win but after a few more drinks I looked at the napkin and realized their cabin was directly across the yard from mine. Had they been spying on me and my friend with benefits that I gone up there with. My defensive mode came back then subsided again thinking about how my friend and I had purposely left the curtain open hoping to be spied on. Our drinking had always gotten us into trouble. I order two dinners and stumbled back to my cabin.

Lisa, my friend was in the shower and the thought of fucking Miss Jane made my dick hard, so I got in the shower with her and took it out on her, not that I even needed that excuse. She is fine as fuck just not girlfriend material can't take Lisa home to mama. She is a nympho and has no shame in it either. That is my kind of girl to hang out with.

I have known her over 10 years now. As we eat, I told her about the offer, and she seemed more excited than I was. Her big ass tits bounced around under her silk robe because she had to use hand jesters for every conversation. "Go fuck her bro why not if that's what they want. Besides it will help them move forward with their relationship trust me" she encouraged with a mouth full of rice. Speaking from experience, she told me how a cheating wife had asked her to fuck her husband to make up for her infidelity and had helped save her sisters marriage. "Ok I am down she's fucking hot anyway" I added.

I brushed my teeth, and I was getting dressed for the evening "ooh and she has on a little tiny dress on and to top it off the whore heels on just the way you like. I would ask to watch but I might get jealous, I don't know why I kind of feel some kind of way but excited at the same time. "I smacked her pretty round ass, for an Asian girl, her booty is so juicy, "mind your businesswoman give me a kiss". The kiss turned into her asking me to stick my dick in her pussy so Jane could taste her later. That did not take long at all.

Soon as I tapped on the door Jane swung it opened took me by the belt buckle and pulled me in. Before the door even shut behind me my zipper was down. "I am glad you came Shawn" John said from the opposite side of the room. He took a heavy snort of some white powder on the counter then later he came over to where his fiancé was gagging on my now fully erected dick. He handed me a glass filled with Tegula and we banged our chilled glasses. He stroked her hair back “I would have brought you one dear, but you seem to have your mouth and hand full”. When he bent down to kiss her on the forehead with my dick in her mouth. Made me a little nervous but then he went back to the counter another snort then dimmed the lights and took a seat away from us.

Her pretty hazel-colored eyes were locked into mine again. I went to unbutton my pants for her, but she stopped me liking to suck my cock through the zipper I guessed. She stood up pulled her dress over her head and had nothing on underneath. My favorite, I love tattooed naked body she even left her white pumps on. “He is delicious” she said before undressing me and leading me by the hand to the bed.” Lisa is going to love to hear that” I thought. I knew she was at the window across the yard trying to get a good look at what was going on. She is just noisy like that a real voyeur but peeping tom that night. “Baby I am going to suck his big ass black dick a little more ok” she said and before he answered she did exactly that. “You go right ahead love” I heard him do another line.

I gulped my drank down so quick I got a brain freeze. This was strange but so exciting to me. As the evening rolled on, I fucked Jane’s mouth and pussy for about 2 hours. She took a few coke breaks and sipped out of Johns glass before jumping back on my dick, sweating her make up off. “Sexy” John Kept whispering. A time when I was fucking her really hard, I could see his worry and that only made me fuck her harder. I know I am an asshole for that, but I had to make it real for them, right?

Yes, I was weird at first but at one point I forgot he was even there at all. I cummed inside her mouth, and she swallowed she showed her tongue, so I knew it was gone. I went to the bathroom to clean off and then I got back John and Jane were fucking like wild animals there was a pile of twenties that turned out to be five hundred dollars sitting on top of my clothing at the door. I watched as I got dressed as he fucked her and smacked her on random places of her beautiful body like a man possessed. She looked into me again and moaned: "oh, shit Shawn" and he pulled her by the hair made her eyes forward and beat her mercilessly. This was truly sexy and with a new boner coming on I had to get back to Lisa.

Morris the moral of the story is my friend with some communication you can have a very sexual relationship have your cake and eat it too. It sounds like you and your ex-wife made some mistakes that you should have learned from. I wish you and your girlfriend lots of luck and lust. Enjoy her be honest and open to get what you want and what she likes out of the relationship. And if you need a guy to pound her sweet ass to get you there, hey I am all about community services you know how to reach me man, for real. Oh, and tell the ex-wife I am looking to have a chat with her and if you don't mind, I want to get and make a few stories for the next book. I hope that's cool Mr. Morris I will send videos if you would like.

Dona, 27 Harford, M.D.

The school of the hard knocks just got really real. I just recently received my bachelor's degree in business and let me tell you, I worked really hard for it. I went back to school after having my son a little while back. My family pitched in so when he turned 3, I was able to go back. His dad decided his co-worker had more to offer, so that was that. Now my son could go to school during the day while I did.

The semester started of like any other. I had to catch up to the curriculum and that was truly one hell of an obstacle for me for a while. However, my professor, Mr. Miller pushed me hard and got me into the tutoring programs. Then I squeaked through. 2nd semester. It was a little better but working part time and tending to my son was slowing me down. Even with the end of the program I found it hard to keep up.

It was a rainy cold February morning when Mr. Miller asked me to stay after class after he handed the back an exam with a barely passing grade. "Dona I am not happy with these scores you're getting" I feel like you're not comprehending the material "I explained my situation to him as he paced around close enough for me to smell his mild scented after shave. He was tall with bronzed skin. Even for a 50 something year old guy he was well kept and handsome. His blue eyes where captivating I had to admit. I had never even thought about what I was working with till he stood directly in front of me while I was still seated with his arms crossed over his broad chest. I instinctively traced his dick pattern with my eyes then sat back short winded and bothered by my observations.

He continued talking as if he missed what I was doing. The tingle I have been ignoring for 3 years was now not going to be denied. Then I looked up into his eyes an seemed he was reading my mind, but I might have been my quilt and anxiety. "There are rules about that here you know" he said in an almost inaudible voice" fraternization can cost everyone involved do you understand" The words seem to go down grip my clit. "I am not "he stopped me "call me for the help you need to get caught up ok Dona" he walked out the classroom leaving me feeling embarrassed yet half and so wet.

I know I had to get rid of my panties right away the next class was to start in 10 minutes. The next few days things seem to be back to normal for him anyway. As the day then weeks past, my imagination made it hard to focus. It seemed to me that was Mr. Millers sole intention these days. His cock bulged in his newfound fitted slacks and jeans a lot more if you asked me. Even some of the other girls were making comments about it or so I thought. His biceps and chest seemed so defined when he flexed well ok when he motioned with his hands. Always clean shaven with bright teeth this once non-existent man was all I was thinking about.

"Dona" when I looked up, he and the whole class were looking into my face. "Umm yes, I am sorry can you repeat that "he frowned while the rest chuckled whispered and popped gum. "I would like to see you after class please" he stuck his hands in his pockets and walked back to the chalk board continuing the lesson on economics. I became much more attentive mainly to ignore the pounding in my chest that echoed so harshly in my head. The bell rang and it was time to face the music.

My peers rushed out and it was me and Mr. Miller alone again. I sat up straight trying to be composed as I could be. He was packing up his briefcase in a hurried manner then finally spoke." Dona we will have to hold this off till later, drop by my house around five and bring some notetaking material. He had one of the many apartments that professor her often stayed in during the year. He seemed really in a rush suddenly and not so much looking at me, as he hurried past me.

I was relieved at first then realized he had just invited me to his apartment to further render me helpless and under his power. How was I really going to be able to focus on anything he was going to say to teach me. It was 5:14 and I was just climbing his front porch steps. It took me a little longer than expected to get ready, considering I needed a shower and changed, and I think my freshman roommate has discovered the many uses of versatile shower head. That a story for another time.

But I was in mid-air when Mr. Miller opens the doors before, I could knock. "I "he" turned away looking down into a book without acknowledging me. Realizing my attire may have been a bit inappropriate due to laundry, my low-cut shirt and to short of shorts. Before I could close the door, Miss, I really don't like tardiness it shows lack of responsibility. There was a cold chill in his voice I had never heard before. "I do apologize Mr. Miller" I blurted. He slammed his book shut and looked at me for a while "Dana, it's important to me that you are the best you can be when you leave this institution" his speech went on for a while as he paced around me like a shark. I felt like prey as his eyes where scanning me and I must admit I like it, in a creepy sort of way.

I clutched my notebook close to my chest listening to him speak. "it's my duty to do everything I can to see that you succeed in the profession with what you're learning in my course do you understand"? He stood behind me, close enough to realize he had on after shave and chocolate on his breath. "Ye-yes sir" I stammered out. "Good now I want you to tell me what else I can do to help you focus? I didn't understand the question, so I said so "I don't understand". He stepped closer and that's when I felt Mr. Millers hard dick on my ass.

I have noticed you measure my cock with your eye's young lady. My heart leaped while my pussy pulsed with excitement "I don't" The words were caught in my throat when he kissed my neck. "I want out of your mind; we will do this and just get you back on track" This white man was smooth as ice. He reached around and took my notebook from me and tossed it to the ground. Now pick it up. The chill returning to his voice again. I bent over at the waist doing as he said. "Tardiness will not be excepted, is that clear"? he asked as he let his dick lay between my ass cheeks now. "Yes sir" I couldn't believe how bold Mr. Miller was and dam did it feel good to be under his control and instruction. "

You will remove your panties now and hand them to me" The words ran through body almost knocking me over, but I did as he asked then he started his circling again. I took off my red laced thongs and shyly handed them to him. He stepped in front of me and snatched them. "Is this proper attire young lady?" he growled. His eyes were dark with lust and a seriousness that made my heart skip a beat. One pace at a time he had barked orders to remove article of clothes till I was ass naked in nothing but my furry Ugg boats. He took me by the hand to his leather couch, part of the sectional that wrapped around the small living room. "Sit Down "The combination of anticipation and the coolness of the lacey material made my nipples harden long before I was ordered to sit down.

He stepped in front of me looking down into my eyes. Without another command. I knew just what he wanted me to do now. I get what it was I was after. I eagerly undid his belt and let his pants drop around his ankles I stared at his dick through his briefs. His dick wasn't big as my baby dad's but he sure as hell wasn't a shrimp like, I always had white guys in my mind pegged to be. His hands were massaging my tits I so needed that. I slowly pulled his fat dick out as he asked and stroked him to his full length. It was a chubby creamy shaft with a thick meaty head on it. Although it was a new feel, all in all it felt good in my hands. I was wondering how it would feel in my mouth and pussy.

Isn't this what you wanted to study instead of the consumer report Dona? He stuck his finger in my mouth after fingering the pre cum from his dicks tip to her fingertips for me to taste him. And it was fucking great. Fuck Dona that tongue feels amazing. But first I have my own desires. I have never been this close to such a young black pussy before lean back! I did as he asked reluctantly. He spread my thighs wide and hung one of my thick legs over his shoulders still wearing his shirt and tie my pussy was on super soaked.

The whole situation had me so fucking hot. I palmed my tits and sucked my own nipples as his gingers parted my sticky lips. My swollen clit twinged with excitement it had been a whole year since anybody had been this close to her. Sure, I had a lil rabbit toy my best friend got me a little while ago. I had replaced the battery in that thing 44 times since then. The sensations were ripping through me. The warmth of his breath teased my opening. I clenched my nipples one at a time as his two fingers slowly plunged in and out of me. Waxing huh, there's no way you be this soft, I could hear his approval. I thought I might have been a little self-conscious being undone by this man.

My body wasn't really where I want all it to be, but he didn't seem to be minding at all. "it's naturally this way" I whispered. "Good his fingers continued to disappear and reappear glistening then disappearing again, then he flicked my clit with his tongue, sending a surg of electricity through by body. He kept right on flicking and sucking at it. And now thrusting much deeper and much more eager fingers into my tight pussy two then three fingers." Shit professor, yes"! I was screaming. He just kept right on. I bit my nipples to muffle my cries, but it was useless. Every touch stroke was like a volt of electricity. I felt my walls tightening around his fingers. I grab the back of his head and begun grinding his face till I had spilled empty, and my breath returned to normal. "That is a very good student" he was really having his way with me.

He bent over the arm of the couch he was relentlessly pounding into me and spanking me wildly, he made me recite formulas to equals that got me spanked and fucked harder with every correct answer. "That's it your learning" he proclaimed. It wasn't too long before he was dripping his cum all over my tits telling me how well I would do in his class.

The rest of the week we couldn't even look at each other in the classroom but all of my assignments and quizzes had high scores. And maybe if I would have given him some more pussy and head, shit I might have even let him stuff his dick in my ass. Either way I have graduated and now on the way to wall street with a degree and very much on time these days. Mr. Miller you have thought me so much. "Age is nothing, but a number and good dick comes in multi colors, oh and the customer is always right!

Alex: way to get ahead Dona!!! That is what I call serious study sessions. Mr. Miller I really do encourage you to really do what you must to keep our systematic observers focused and attentive by any means necessary. By the way the very first chance I get to fuck a woman in her furry Ugg's I am so doing it. That's not too far from my high heel fetish. And to my preggers and new moms a real man knows good pussy lies with the women guys just refuse to pull out of. So, if somebody makes you feel like you're not sexy with those wide hip's fuller lips and swollen tits during and after telling him to fuck off and come find me or any other sensible man. And as always, we mature men keep scoring with the young ladies in all walks of life.

~~I think I moved and didn't delete~~

~~Pg 6 H~~

~~So, while you may be aggressively seeking and wrecking homes of those who moments of weakness for a pretty face and body, just issues and those who just can't seem to get their wives to be as nasty as Nancy. There still is a great bunch of good healthy relationships out there. I personally, if and only if I was claiming to be in a relationship with anyone. She would be down with us~~

~~bringing home a nympho here and again, no time to be a creep. It ain't fun if the homie ain't getting none. My lady has to be my homie, a comrade of mine before she got a ring outta me.~~

~~Whoever it is that you're in love with may see or know about the shit you do, men talk too much and may be there reason he keeps you away. You ever consider not being a huntress. I'm not hating or loving, in fact very interested in your life style. I just have to put these thoughts into context for our readers. As I say often, "live life to the fullest" just try to be the best at what you do and avoid doing anything you'll regret in the future. And please keep an eye out for the "Huntress Slayers" I'm telling you, there are really out there snooping around, and might show up at your door step, my love!~~

~~Pg 5 H~~

Are all probably the most hatred if other women know. Your “huntresses”, am, I right? I sure you’re getting plenty of play too. There’s plenty of husbands out their board with that wife that won’t try new things. The wife that doesn’t suck a dick or at least learning should not even have gotten a second date never the less a ring and a last name. fuck that? Plus, you have those guys that are sex addicts “players” with cash to burn. I have a friend that just had to see if he still had to see if he still had to see if still had it, plus his wife is a true fucking nag. I actually recommended that he fuck his slutty porn star looking neighbor. Just to get it out his system and save his marriage and the expensive break up. That’s called “using your head”.

Ebony, look a nasty girl like any red blood new in the world. I just hope you’re being safe and not exposing your daughter to the fuck shit you do. Take what you’re doing serious if it is your sport and do not, repeat do NOT tease or throw what you do in either women’s faces. That’s what could make shit wild and dangerous. Take my advice on that love. In closing; go to say not all husbands can be got some wives care just so fucking awesome their men can’t wait to get home to them.

~~You wake up one day and realize you can't at. Your age and if my imagination of your body is on point, fucking is going to be a sport you great at right now. best part is you can get even better. I like the whole "huntress" idea. You said, have been spotted by one of your pack, huh? Now I am wondering who it could be. And where she sees me with "PYT" pretty young thing. Those reading waiting to read the lines into deep personals, keep reading. I will give a little here and there. But back to miss Ebony miss snatch your man. Are you keeping tabs on me?~~

~~Now on the after end of this all you point out some of the ladies may be upset with your forgetting their husbands. That is a very serious worry you may want to tread carefully around. I have known some very vicious ladies in my day that will fuck you up about their man's dick in your mouth, physically or metaphorically.~~

Albert. M.

29 Baltimore, MD

My girlfriend Martha and I have been dating for about a full year now. She is alright, I guess. She's a full figured Indian and Polish girl. 26 years old, nice ass, 28 D tits pouty lips and blue/green eyes. Our love for back-to-back orgasms and cooking brought us together, no question there. Aside from that I find that our communication really sucks. Besides money, I don't trust her at all when it comes to loyalty. She fucked a few guys; I knew back in the days while she was already in a relationship with another guy. I have even had her own family tell me she was bad news.

That brings me to her little sister, she's only 19 but much more reasonable. Recently, I found myself confiding in her about things and maybe it's why I've had the urges to bone the shit out of her. She's your average 19-year-old, body wise, really slim maybe 140 pounds, small features not at all curvy as her sister is but the lips must be a family trait. She hasn't ever dated a black guy. But she says she's interested. Not in me, but the idea, you know.

Anyway, I caught her drinking at a party and what started off as a scolding by me ended up going different. She was wearing a low-cut shirt and a pair of tiny shorts that night. When I got there, right away, asked her to come and speak to me outside. We went back and forth about her being at this party and the way she was dressed. There was a jealous rage, you know, inside of me like she was my girl. "I'm grown" she kept saying. She did live on her own, drive and work and had been since high school unlike her sister who still lives at home with mom and dad.

We got in my car to avoid making a big scene. The bulge in my jeans must have snuck up on us just then because the conversation went right if "is your dick hard right now?!" she asked shocked. I looked down. Before, I could respond she reached over and stroked my dick through my jeans. "Don't lie that your dick is super hard." She slurred and continued to stroke drunkenly. Our egos were desperate, and I was speechless. "You want to fuck me don't you" I never heard her speak like this it must have been the punch talking but my dick jumped under her hand. "Yes, but I can't" neither one of us stopped the contact. Something had to happen quickly to stop this because I felt pre-cum starting to seep through the material. “I think you really want to fuck me.” With that she got out of the car and back into the party. I couldn’t believe what just happened. Not that I wouldn’t fuck a younger girl but not my girl’s sister. Well, I did not think so anyway.

I calmed myself down and went back in really to see if she was telling anyone. But she wasn’t her and her friend were dancing, laughing, and goofing off, we made quick eye contact but that was it all night. I even drove her home she had had too much to drink. She slept, as I drove, and when she got to her apartment, she gave me the usual kiss on the check and went inside. Since then, we’ve still have been having deep conversations but never again any contact. It was like it never happened at all.

Me and her older sister don’t really speak that often about anything important, but the sex is great. Little sister is still on my fuck list quite as kept. But with her it more about the connection and a lot less physical is my fantasy of fucking her a bad thing? I mean I do plan on trying to make things better with my girlfriend. We’ve made some break throughs, trust wise, I guess. She has recently come out and told me the truths about some things in the past that she kept lying about. I don’t know if it’s one of her many tricks to con me into thinking she is worthy of my time. Even her little sister warns me not to be too invested. But then again little sister here could be waiting for chance to get all my attention and cock to herself. Who knows?

After Martha. Told me about her “mistakes”, I felt like I could make a few of my own. She owed me a few, am I right here? No good deed should go unpaid is that not the rule. Her sister just turned 20 and she is still growing but her mom seems to like to be close to me too. Martha has never done anything with anyone, that I know of personally and maybe that's why, I have not done what my dick is telling me every time I am around her family members. Of course, I don't tell her little sister these things although we speak about everything including our sex lives. That has gotten me near meltdown panic, I will admit. But I keep it together thinking it's getting better, for real. Martha is offering up more everyday though. Our sex has never been better, sure her mom or sisters' images may replace hers in certain light, but she has that "yummy" that dude Justin sings about so what can I say. In time I'll learn to love and her trust her, right?

Alex: Well, a man can dream but if you act on this you may not be able to come back, and even worst if good pussy is another family trait. It will get out eventually and you will be cut off. If they live by the "blood is thicker than water" motto. I'm a big fan of communication too, so I feel you on the attraction but if all boils down to where you see yourself going with big sister. If it's a short-term fuck, I would go for its bro, but if you are saying you're "working on it" you should avoid any unneeded issues. They will only do more harm than good.

Keep little sister on the fuck list but only as a vengeance pawn. If big sister goes back to her old ways kill two birds one bone. Try to remember another important motto "once a whore always a whore." It's hard for them to just stop it cold turkey. Keep your eyes open on this one in some very rare case, I have found some do change for the better other, the majority, just get good at hiding it the older they get. The woman is a secretive creature in general when there loving that promiscuous lifestyle. Protect yourself and having that small insurance policy may make you feel better too, it is okay to be careful of a girl that is unsteady in that area of her life.

I have accidentally dated a few myself and I always wished I did the dirt to them first or kept an insurance policy that guaranteed me quick immediate revenge, so I know what you mean. These days the understanding that it's the lies their selves that do the most damage not really the action. It's all the creeping and sneaking to do what you did, is the hurtful part. Trust is primary in a relationship without it you have nothing at all. "Dating" means collecting data on someone you're being intimate with in anyway. So, make sure fellas and ladies you protect self-first. No matter how good the sex is, guard your hearts. I have learned there is good pussy all over the planet it's like air.

> You only have one little heart don't let it suffer to many damages. Use the head on your shoulders Albert or you will be sorry. And you need to keep in mind a young girl is going to explore regardless so know some things come with the territory, okay. Martha may not be ready to open up, afraid of your judgement, go be easy on your approach and shit might just get better and who knows you might just change a ho after all, but probably not.

This one is a story from my early years in Philadelphia when I had come back from school in Morganfield, Kentucky, I wrote it down thinking "print worthy" I was hoping to do something with this someday and now I can.

Alex: I moved back home after a bad break up with my on again off again slut of a girlfriend. Anyway, my parents hadn't moved a thing in my room. It was like they had always imagined I'd come back to my room in the attic. My cards, old posters of Harley Davidson Bikes and Chicks from Baywatch. My telescope still in the window aimed at the big dipper. Only thing that was different was that I was taller now, so the ceiling seemed so much lower causing me to duck and bunch in certain parts of the room where the roof was pitched downward. I started to move things around, adding and removing things, they I saw her.

It was Mrs. Bennett my neighbor. Growing up I remember having the biggest crush on this lady but that was 8 years ago, and she was in her 40's then but even now at 55 she was still fucking hot. From what I had hear Mr. B had kicked the bucket in their bedroom 3 years ago that's probably why she had moved her bedroom to the side of the house that I was just looking into. She was bent overlooking for something in a dress drawer. She was wearing a pair of white yoga leggings that made her very large ass look even more defined and from here it didn't look like she was wearing any panties. From this angle I could only see her from the back, but a mirrored reflection on the other side of the room allowed me a quick peek down her sports bra. She was wearing a headband and her dirty blonde hair was tied back in a messy ponytail is all I could catch before she ran out again. She must be doing her workouts still, I remember she had been doing that since I was way younger, my mom tried it out with her but soon quit.

My family was the only black family on this side of the street yet and still we had the respect of the neighbors. My family worked hard to make no troubles here. I grew up here so I guess that would explain my deep desires for white women, but I have no valid reason to why I love the cougar type. They must be older; in 8th grade I dated a girl in college. And now that I think about it, girls my age never really worked out. Perfect example my ex was 23 but messy with no chill or manners. She had to go. When I was 15, I snuck a secret admirer note into Mrs. Bennett's mailbox while she was out jogging one morning before going to church. I imagined she'd give me a kiss, but it never happened but a kids got to have dreams, right? Anyway, I finished unpacking but Mrs. Bennett's 5'4" frame and all her curves kept popping in my head. It has always amazed me how her ass and tits probably made up most of her weight, made her shaped like an hourglass, no matter how modest she dressed she couldn't hide that figure and now that I was older, I guess I could really appreciate that a lot more.

I was out running a few errands for my mom, and I swear it was like milf central all-around town. Maybe it was just me, but it seemed like there was a serious influx of sexy women in my small area suddenly. Then again, I had been gone a while. I preferred white women. But don't get it confused I don't discriminate so seeing a few older black and even Spanish women in the market's, a middle eastern milk at the post office had also caught my attention.

When I got home my mom was outside talking to fine ass Mrs. Bennett who was looking like she had just come from one of her vigorous runs. She had sweat glistened on her skin and with her hands on her hips the way she had them now made her stand wide and giving me a perfect front view that I will lock in my mind forever.

I hit the key fob locking the door to my Tahoe. I played cool and pretended to not be aware of them by looking inside the bags I was carrying. “And there he is now” my mom giggled. I looked up with a faint smile “what I do this time?”, half joking. “Wow look at you Alexander, all grown up into a fine young man, haven’t you?” Mrs. Bennett asked. I smiled and said hello and the two of them spoke at me like a baby just learning to walk. All I could do I smile and take in Mrs. B’s beauty and not try to be obvious. Your mother was telling me how great you are at helping her out. So, if it isn’t way too much to ask or maybe I could pay you to help me with some of the heavy-duty things here and there. Shoot you could make a business out of it, there aren’t many youngens around here, willing to work anyways. I could sure use the money and being around Miss B wouldn’t be bad either, I thought to myself. “Sure, Miss B” I said at my mother’s already nodding approval. Just let me know, I said turning on my heels heading to the house before my eyes groped this woman’s large tits, again her flat creamy belly was exposed do to her wearing the short tank top. The sweat that ran down her body had now collected to the front of her leggings making her chubby pussy hard to ignore. I had to get away from there, ASAP.

"It was nice seeing you again Miss B need me just call me over and get my mom to give you the number to reach my cell" She took a firm grab at my arms and promised to do just that. Her touch seemed to send a chain of lust through my body. I sat the bags down and went to take a shower, while I jerked off till the water ran from steamy to cold.

Later that evening after dinner I went to the window in my room to see if I could catch a glimpse of Mrs. Bennett before I watched a movie. And there she was totally in the nude. Her body even more perfect than I could have ever imagined. A few tan lines and wet hair made her look even more seductive. Her nipple where a light blush shade of pink just like her lips. And she had her pussy trimmed so neatly. I almost thought it was bald. This woman kept it together over the years there was no denying that.

Instantly my dick started to rise and though I felt wrong for prying in on Mrs. Bennett I couldn't draw myself to stop it. She slowly lotion herself careful to hit every spot she bent over in the mirror to get her tattooed ankles and that was the first time I had seen the two dimples on her lower back. My heart rate sped up; my dick felt like it was about to tear threw my jeans. I went to grab my office desk chair and when I got back, her window was dark, the show was over. A television shined different hues of lights in there, but her bed was not in my view, and I cursed my luck and desperation at the same time. Why did this lady have to be so fucking sexy, so desirable, and so close that I couldn't resist her sight?

A week of peeping later, she asked me to run a few errands for her and cut the grass and a series of other things. On one occasion I saw the pair of lacy front hot pink thongs that had slipped out of a drawer or something one day, there it laid on her bed. I don't know why but I needed to feel them. I know she was downstairs when I picked them up and bringing them to my face when a thought entered my head "maybe I could take them." That's when I heard my name in a low voice from behind me "now Alex", I spun around and there she was with a hurt scowl on her face "I'm ----" she cut me short and snatched her underwear out of my hand.

This is private" she said through her gritted teeth. A side of Mrs. Bennett I've never known. All I could do was stand there dumbfounded while she rightfully scolded me and my trespass. "How would you like it if I did it to you, in fact take your pants off." I thought I was losing it till I looked in her sky-blue eyes and she said it again much more serious "take them off Alexander, now!"

I hurried my jeans off to keep her voice down. She walked over and took a handful of my dick and balls with a grip that bordered danger pleasure. My heart pounded double time at the mix of the feelings of fear and excitement. My cock stupidly swelled in her grasp increasing both the danger and pleasure. Oh, so you have not learned manners and obviously you're a man so letting your mother handle this is out of the questions, take it all off and lay the fuck down don't let move a muscle boy.

I never heard her ever use this tone before. I was scared of what was to come once she left the room. The she returned with rope and tied my hands together quickly and roughly to her headboard. She looked into my eyes intently as she made her knot, tied professionally without missing a beat. Then slapped me across the face, "there, that should do it." The sting was minimal but still shocking, she was gone again. My dick was semi hard as I laid tied up. My mind couldn't really fathom what Mrs. Bennett would do next.

Twenty minutes later she returned in a figure fitting silk lingerie style robe with a deep V. In case you're thinking someone will come for you, I let your mom know you had to run across town to see a friend and left your phone here, that she now has. My nerves got really bad, how long was she planning on keeping me here? She turned her back to me and went rummaging through the dresser. I watched her so many times bend over at from my window. She came up with an arm full of her panties. These are what you like right and threw them all over me. You better answer me she said softly but nervously. "Yes mam" I hesitated; she said good.

Then pulled her robe slowly open, staring a hole into me. Her body was even more magnificent up close, and my dick stood up acknowledging this fact. "Alex, how long have you wanted to fuck me, and you better be honest if you know what is good for you. With her hand on her hips again. Since I was a boy, 15 or so, I can't remember, I spat out surprising myself. "hmm" she sang going into a walk-in closet, a few moments later I could hear steps against the hardwood floor she appeared in a pair of red tie up high heels. The hoe ones that let her pedicured toes peak out. Her legs seem to go on forever as her four-inch heels stabbed the ground.

Like my dick wasn't hard enough. "You boys like these don't you she said into the mirror as she checked herself out." All I could do was admire her beauty. Even the veins that popped out on her feet, her large heavy breast, still firm, heart shaped ass, and her tight abs that made her pussy look like a soft trimmed mound I needed to land into.

She took rushed steps over to me that made her heavy tits bounce with each stride. When she reached me, she grabbed my throat? "You will answer me, do you boys like these or not?" Her grip was fierce, "Yes" I choked out. When she let me go, I found myself gasping for air, yet my dick was still very much excited. She raised a foot from the ground and put it on my chest. The heel cutting into my skin, but God was it turning me the fuck on the way she was handling me. It was making my whole-body tingle I just wanted to get lose and take her right then and there. "Kiss my foot," I hesitantly obliged, Mrs. B positioned it in a low angle so my wet tongue would go where she wanted "that's a good boy" she stepped down and smacked my standing twelve-inch dick so hard pre-cum lightly splashed all over my belly. "Oh, no worst" she moaned then she licked my stomach until it was all gone. She never losing eye contact with me. I swear I thought I would explode.

I'll be drinking you Alex for as long as you have been thinking of fucking me. I was lost, only for a short while until she made it clear you for a while now have fucked me your eyes. Since you were knee high, in high school too. You have been home only a few days and you have sat up there watching my naked body, watching a dead man's wife putting up and remove her stockings, panties, bras, and make up. Just greedily taking advantage of poor old Miss Bennett, haven't you?" How could she have known? Her intentions were evil and treacherous. Are you jerking that being young black dick of yours up there when you're looking at my ass and pussy from up there? She asked with a sly smile "yes", I told the truth. "And what do I get, just used?".

In your mind I'm fucked and sucking your dick then left, right? Oh no I don't think so. I like to cum just as much as the next guy. Beside you get off, shouldn't I? I know you've got better manners then that. Her statement would have knocked him down if he were not already laying down on her soft king size bed. "You are tied up cause it's my turn, understand?" I nodded, she smacked me again, much hard this time. "You will be polite and answer when spoken to is that understood?" Damn her. "Yes mam".

My dick wouldn't stop pulsing at her wickedness. "Any questions?" I thought then asked, "Are you going to fuck me?" She didn't answer, instead she climbed on the bed with her heeled feet and stood over top my face, one handheld her steady using the wall and headboard while the other began rubbing her clit and popping her manicured fingers into her soaked pussy.

She was getting so much pleasure in resisting my touch and it was agonizing to me. In and out she went. Suddenly I felt tiny sprinkles of her juices drizzling on my face. I opened my mouth in hope to catch some since she wouldn't let me get the direct drink or taste I needed. "Ahh shit yes, yes, yes" she panted looking down at me without warning she sat on my face, so I began licking her pussy to ass as she slid back and forth. Damn she tasted so fucking good I just wanted to inhale her. Hearing her moan and demand I eat that ass was truly riveting.

She stood back up and kept on doing what she was "you are my captive for three days a week, you will do as I please for your crimes against me" I went to talk but she stuffed my mouth with one of her black lacy thongs. "I wasn't asking" she continued popping her pussy this time more vigorously with one foot on my chest. Her juices ran down her legs and all over me as she squirted. "Ahh fuck yah shit, I'm Cumming for you, fuck, fuck!" she screamed. She removed the panties from my mouth and replace them with her two soaked fingers, her taste was like honey "now, I will give your more as soon as your done cutting the grass." She sashayed away for few minutes leaving me in flames. She returned showered and dressed and untied me. I know she would only shame me and denied me access if I tried. "You will be a good boy won't you" I agreed to be, so she kissed my lips. "Mowers in the garage."

This has been going on few months too. Sure, she paid well and lets me watch her through my window, but I don't know if I can just be okay with this for too much longer, I just had to figure out what it would take get her mouth or pussy on my dick? I mean sure I know I started this but enough was enough. I truly had a dilemma here. She's a woman and an experience one at that. This can really go so many ways. In reality though I did kind of violate her first. But it sounded like she's been okay with it until I actually made personal contact in her zone. "Never venture off into a lionesses cave." I had been told this many times before.

On the bright side she had taught me self-control and the act of eating pussy. Fellas, it is an art, women all over the world tell me about men who give them bad head. "One must be one with the V's Chee." LOL. But practice, practice, practice makes perfect. One of my home girls taught me everything I knew as I taught her what she needed. We had nothing to really worry about with each other we could tease and criticize without consequences. But Miss B was a serious master of the art. Miss B could have been so gracious to let me explore her a tad further if I made myself less available.

One morning I went over and told her I quit and walked away in a hurry. I ignored her calls; bluffing was out of the question. I let her see me jerk off, maybe she breaks or I will threaten to move out even. I kept my curtain closed, she had to have noticed. It was a Sunday morning and the bell rung while my mom was out. When I opened the door Miss B was covered in sweat from her run. "Ok come get what you want tonight at eight, better not be late!" Before I could respond she had her back turned and walking slowly away enough for me to notice the bounce of her round ass was not restricted by any underwear. I love stretch pants on women with nice asses like Miss B's. She bent over to pick up some fresh meal from her porch that made the chubbiness of her twat even more desirable. This was one of her tricks and I just could not allow her to win. I closed the door quickly so she would look back and think maybe that her spell had not worked. But the throbbing in my chest and boxers said otherwise. I only had two hours to figure out how I was going to play this. I made my myself cum to a few videos of Kelly Stax getting fucked like the whore she was, always a reliever that bitch. Thanks Kelly.

After a shower I was ready, my plan, I felt was a solid one. I walked past the mirror in the hallway before going to the front door and said, "my turn, again." I went to knock on the side door as always but tonight it was left cracked open a. bit. I had to stay calm and in control to get through this as a victor. "Miss B" I yelled out over the famous "what's love got to do with it" track that the amazing Tina Turner made so famous. As I walked towards the kitchen, there was in another pair of heels all white with her short China girl silk robe, barely covering her ass. She was bent over into the stove wagging her ass and singing along with the Queen of pop. I stood there and simply admired her from this distance. She had the table set in the dining room dishes and silverware and two glasses of wine. "Excuse me miss" came on next, but she had spun around. "You keep making a habit of breaking into here don't you sir." Her smile told me she forgave me and was happy to see me. "Come here and give mama a kiss."

I walk over and gave her a deep tongue kiss while I palmed her ass. This was new, we didn't do things like this from the beginning it had been her aggressive demands nothing as intimate as this. "Dinner will be ready in a few bring me that glass of wine while you wait. We drank a few glasses before and after the lamb chop three course meal she prepared. We had light conversation and a few laughs. She told me how she had not been entered since Mr. Bennett had died "it was a rare occasion as it was." She brought out ice cream and I couldn't stop imagining the pleasure she seemed to be delaying tonight. I took the dishes to the sink and when I returned, she was ready.

At some point she shed her robe and was waiting in the doorway, her luscious body never seemed to stop confounding me. She let me kiss her neck, a lick, a suck, pinch, and relish her divine sexy nipples. She undid my belt and as soon as it was undone, she slowly went down to her knees making sure she had my attention. Our eyes were locked to each other's again while she handled my rod with the swiftness of a specialist. Miss B's mouth was moist and had enough pressure to keep my attention. She took almost the whole twelve inches at first and that was truly an astonishing feat, until she really did it. This time she got my dick so far in her throat she actually stuck her tongue out and licked the underside of my balls. Only for them to roll to the back of my head, did we ever break eye contact. We got into a rhythm I gently pushed in and out of her slippery mouth. I had her ponytail trapped around my fist like I had seen done so long ago in the magazine. I put one foot up on top of the dining room chair cushions, so she had better access to my balls. Instead, she grabbed both my ass cheeks with her hands so she could pull me forward with plenty roughness now into her veracious plumped lips. So much of this was new to me especially when she began slapping my ass. I must admit, strange but simply invigorating.

I needed to give her all of me and now sure I had gotten thousands of blow jobs but never like this. She got ever more intense in the living room. With careful and very delicate strokes at first, I parted the folds of her treasure. It was the first time I noticed fear in Miss B's eyes "you okay" I asked hoping I wasn't hurting her. She did not respond instead she pulled me forward burying me deep inside of her warmth. "Oh shit, you a bad boy" she whispered "this is what you wanted so take it, just take it" she kept whispering with her most sultry moan in my ear. I dug deeper making her cry out then speed up until our skin slapping might be able to be heard across the street. Her nails felt sharp, yet oh so good digging into my back and ass cheeks. With her legs on my shoulders, I felt powerful and mighty. She looked into my eyes still demanding I "take" what I came for without hesitations I did just that. I spent the evening eating and entering her till she was exhausted, and I drained all of any fluids and powers to even continue. That was the last time we ever touched.

The next day when I got the mail, there was a large manila envelope in my mailbox with no return address but addressed to me. "A CERTIFICATE OF ACHIEVEMENT Alex Pain" "My dear you are truly an over achiever. I have installed into you the art that keep hearts. Remember your teachings and never forget your teacher. Take care in life and keep in mind your manners, mind your business, and mind your manners. You too have taught me a few things…Love, Mrs. B."

There was a moving truck shutting the back door. It was chilly morning, but I had to know what was going on. That's when she honked, driving by waving and blowing me a kiss and nothing else since. There was a gain I could not make heads or tails of it at first when I text then called her number and realized her phone number had been changed. Heart break. That summer I moved out after the coldest winter ever. My mother said Miss B's house went up for sale and that it was it. All lessons have been retained and never forgotten Miss B. I hope you read this and know that I am very appreciative for the courses in passion. I have put my skills to good use. The women in my life really owe you, the thanks for the many over the top orgasms I have given them. Nevertheless, my lady I am still under your spell, should you decide your lawn needs my touch just direct me.

Falisha O, 40

Baton Rouge, LA

I hope I'm not being ridiculous hoping you print this but Alex we had great times and I wish shit was different. There is no denying you've given me orgasms unmeasurable by natural means. The way you "beat the box" boy will have me forever ready to find you. My husband still brings up our affair in arguments 'til this day. But he'll never understand what you did for us. Honestly if it was not for our drunken trades on Bourbon Street, I'm sure I would have been let go by him. I had fought to keep our home together for so long, but did he care? That tramp from his office seemed to be all he was interested in. That video of you fucking me in the ass like a mad man on my 35th birthday, that he found in my phone really made a world of difference. I mean shame on me for not warning you about him, but you handled yourself quite well that night. Then the way you punished me by force fucking my throat and stretching all of my holes before you left has made me quiver at the thought, ever since. If you are ever in town how about we have a few of those Hurricanes and you give me a few back shots. I'll do that thing.

Last September I thought I fell in love with a lady cop. At first, I was making a pass on the wrong side of a semi, then when she stopped me, I could not resist making a pass at her. She may have been only five foot seven if that, jet black hair, and even with no make-up her facial features were stunning. Her serious demeanor made her dolphin-colored eye even more extremely stunning. Of course, my license was still suspended.

When she came back from her cruiser with my papers, she asked me to step out of the car. Maybe it was about my license or my inability to stop looking at her belt buckle, okay under her belt buckle. It was the V down there kept calling me to it. I had not noticed it 'til she walked away with my credentials the first time. I happen to look in the rear-view mirror and realized how ample ass this woman had. “Dammmmm” I moaned. I was sure you could see it from the front. For a second, she looked over her shoulder and I think she caught me starring. When she directed me to the back of my car obviously unshaken by my physical appearance like most smaller white law enforcement officers are. She patted me down with my consent, “please don’t find it” I prayed, then she did, my dick was so damn hard. I knew her hand would find it but eventually if she was going to do her training to make sure I wasn’t a threat to her. “what’s---“then she stopped. “Sir are you aware your license is suspended?” She asked me instead. “Yes, mam. It will be restored in a few days I just had to make a run to the store really quick for my hungry mom.” I lied. “Sir there was cigarettes, whip cream, energy drinks, a case of Heineken’s, a large box of condoms, and I think baby oil. Now unless your mom has the oddest appetite I have ever heard of, or you just lied to me.” Strike two. You want to push for the third? She dared me in her very serious official tone. “I’m sorry, just nervous.” They say beauty disarms but that was not the case here.

I needed to be careful. She was not the average cutie with a booty. Her great rack underneath her vest and khaki colored uniform refused to be subdued and kept my eyes wandering down to her badge then name tag, but I knew I had to chill out before she put me on ice. “Look I’m going to sight you for the license, I will ask you to let me follow you home and not drive until your legal to do so, when you come to court and you better” She took a step closer fisting her small hand around the pen she was holding making my heart pound a bit. If you at that time, have it all cleaned up, I may toss the ticket before we go into court, got it? Our eyes were in each other's scanning for what at the time I don't know "yes, I got it."

My dick got even harder knowing she had given me a small, but very appreciated hall pass. As promised, she escorted me home. She waited until I got my "groceries" out and locked the doors. "You make sure to feed your mom sir, see you at court." She said with a faint yet pretty smile before making a U-turn. I took her advice, stayed off the road 'til I got cleared, and that morning when I got to the courthouse, I almost didn't recognize her 'til she called my name. She wore a very fitting pair of blue jeans that shamelessly showed off her bountiful curves, a white button up blouse and what must have been a bra made of cloud the way her full breast bounced around almost threw what had to be buttons made of titanium or some other strong material. Random piercing in her ear and her tongue really surprised me. She even had on a touch of make-up and lip gloss on.

"Have you got your affairs in order Mr. Pain?" Still stern but even more sexy to me, "yes mam, I do" she took the documents from the Department of Motor Vehicles and when she was satisfied handed them back "wait here please." She walked away and made sure to catch me again staring at her wonderful back side. This time I was certain she caught me looking she shook her head in shame at me as she disappeared in an office in the hallway. When she returned, I had not been able to yet talk down Mr. Nasty, he hardly ever listens to me anyway. And maybe I had not noticed it before but there were two buttons undone. She had to have just done that. There was no way I would have missed that fluffy tanned flesh I was seeing, just no way.

“Ok Pain, all good, now you can wine and dine me to thank me.” I thought my ears were playing trick on me “Really?” I was shocked by the women’s boldness and even more by my eagerness. “Are you disobeying my orders Pain?” There was no way I was going to miss this opportunity “lead the way madam.” And she spun on her heels and did just that. She stopped at her car opened the trunk and bent into it giving me a full view of juicy ass before coming out with a duffle bag. I tried to look away but at this point I didn’t think I had to. She walked right up to me this time; her breast firm yet soft against me. “Mr. Pain I should warn you that I too have a very odd appetite!”

At the time I don’t think she knew I aimed to please just as much as I didn’t know the pleasure she required was on a new level. We had two Heinekens and ordered to Jack Daniels pork barbeque dinners to go. The conversation was cool. She was just more relaxing and ever easier on the eyes too off duty. She was 28, mother of three with a failing marriage. This guy was mentally abusive and lacked libido anymore. “Maybe it’s my weight” She pouted playfully. “Hell no” I assured her that a real man is always going to want a little extra meat on his plate. We laughed and when our orders came, she demanded she drive. If that was what she called it anyway, because she pushed my Range Rover up to a hundred miles per hour on the highway then every bit of eighty maybe ninety on the back roads to my house. I cringed with every sharp maneuver she made. I was glad when we came to a stop in my driveway. “Don’t be scared now we're just getting started Mr. Pain." She nearly grinned with smile I couldn't resist.

She insisted she carry her own bag. Once inside she complimented the décor but wanted directions to the shower and my bedroom. "Bring up some wine, and that gun in your pants, I felt the other day." Again, taken but impressed by her forward boldness. "Loaded and cocked madam." I shot back. When she came out of the bathroom she had on a pair of trooper style sunglasses, a tight ponytail, pink fishnets, and high heels. So tall, it seemed about six foot now. A new coat of lip gloss. This women's body was amazing even her C-section scar turned me on. She was sleeved up and even more tattoos ran up and down her legs. Her big ass tits were pierced through her pretty pink nipples. I looked over her carefully even walked around her as she stood there, hands on her hip, enjoying my inspection. "I guess you do have the right to remain silent" She teased. The smell of the Chanel #9 was light but intoxicating. At the point Mr. Nasty was too eager to come out and play.

I needed to be in control, so I poured glasses of wine, "I'll be back." I walked downstairs, hoping to shake it off by the time I got back to her but grabbing the whipped cream and baby oil excited me even more. But it wasn't 'til I came back, and Mrs. Officer was laying legs wide open on the king size bed and using her knight stick in her asshole while making circles with her fingers on her clit moaning. A drink, well I gulped down two glasses of wine and watched her get off at least three times. The fact she had kept her glasses, stockings, and heels on this whole time made me want to keep her for good. When I got naked, I began dripping baby oil on her body making her glisten like a holiday ham. She became braver and braver with her stick going deeper and deeper into her ass only removing it to spit on it. She moaned out loud as if she was alone or just didn't give a fuck she wasn't. I could no longer resist, and Mr. Nasty was no fucking help. Pre-cum began oozing out the tip of my fat mushroom head, "you have wined me now dine me." I stood over her on the bed as she engulfed half of the length of my dick. Aggressively she took ahold of my balls and used them like guiding handlebars to send me in and out of her warm mouth. She was moaning, gagging, and drooling all at the same time.

I took her by her ponytail and slapped her hard across her face for her greed and she welcomed it. "Punish me." She panted like a swimmer coming up for air. I fucked her mouth like a mad man possessed, making her grayish eye well up with tears. I pulled out and took her by the throat, "open your mouth" then spit on it and stuff it with my dick again. The way white women's lips swell after vigorous blow jobs always turns me on. So, I bent her over and suck her dripping pink pussy and tongued whipped cream from her gapped asshole 'til she screamed, "fuck I'm Cumming don't you dare……fucking….stoopppppp." She was drunk of ecstasy like I was.

I laid her flat, sat on her face backwards so I could fuck her enormous tits while she licked my ass, a reservation for my true freaks. And she was every bit that and more. She cuffed me and slapped, scratched, and choked me as she rode my twelve-inch cock. She let me suck her pierced nipples when I begged her too. She would turn around and ride me that way making me desire the left-over cream that was still on her asshole. As her ass opened and shut while she rode my dick backwards. “This is assault of an …. Officer…. Mother fucker.” She moaned when she let me cuff her to the headboard while she was bent doggy style “bitch so what, take this dick” I spanked her hard and fucked her harder. Throughout the madness her glasses stayed on as well as the rest of her gear. The shoes are almost mandatory for me as many of you know and the stockings, I began to temp a little bit but her sweaty, torn up, grungy whore look was really taking over the top.

When I uncuffed her I picked her up draped her legs over my arms ‘til her screams and moans from my harsh pounding made her bit my neck, damn her that was the spot, I put her down on her knees and shot one of the stickiest, messiest, and hottest loads of cum ever all over her glasses, lips, and tits. “Yes, give it to me” she demanded and smacking my dick on her face. Roughest sex is my thing too and with every experience I become more and more open to the possible things of the minds. We are always going to push the limits. That’s just what the human race has always done, is it not? Mrs. Officer and I have continued our escapades throughout the years and have only gotten bolder with the levels of pain in the bedroom. She let me use the loaded 9mm in her recently. It must have been the threat of having her head blown off or something, but she creamed so heavy she claims the gun had to be cleaned twice to get back to the way she liked.

We are into the bondage and submission thing really deep now and I guess when you get to those points sometimes it's hard to turn back. The fantasies are good and when exploring these things with your wife is really going to be fun.

Kevin, 43, Washington, DC

Books where I work are a way out for those there, I'm assuming the first time I read something you wrote was at work suggested in house. I have been a corrections officer for six years now just over the line in Virginia. We don't get paid too much or nearly enough should say to be dealing with the shit we do on a regular basis. But there are some good days. For example, we have a few females, although they are majority males for the most part, we get the washed up and beat down ones in the looks and life department. But there are a few of them who actually recover quickly from the abuses they have been subjected their bodies to: drugs, alcohol, poverty, or all of the above sometime. Their hair returns to its heathy luster, all of the hollows fill back up too. We get them black, white, Spanish, Indian, Asian, or whatever – we don't discriminate in our regional jails.

Danisha, a 53-year-old shop lifter lets me watch her cum on her very creatively designed dildo. She sits up in the corner stark naked and slides the daily newspaper molded into a huge cleverly designed dick layered in saran wrapping, in and out with her issued panties in her mouth. Her skin and even darker nipples look the best when she covered in sweat obviously at it for a while. My presence makes her cum every time. She always silently mouths "thank you" in case anyone is listening. I hope before her ten-and-a-half-month bid is over, she understands the pleasure is all mine. Then there's two women named Kim who are cellmates who I catch regularly in the 69 position. One is thirty-seven, five foot six inches, red hair with big tits and covered in tats like Von-D. The other reminds me of those women from that Love and Hip Hop show they always watch in here. Slim waist extreme ass, perky young tits, and long hair. At. Twenty-eight, and six foot the girl could no doubt stop traffic.

In fact, they were both serving time for prostitution in the area. Watching them just finger each other's pussy and assholes while the rest of the probates is in the yard makes my dick so fucking hard, I swear it feels like it could break. They always make sure to turn it up a notch when I'm watching, for a few candy bars. Lacy, twenty-six, five-foot Mexican girl with a heart shaped ass walked around in her cell down to solitary confinement naked singing songs in only her socks and her hair in two sexy naughty girl ponytails that hang down to her round breast. Her oversized areolas and elongated chocolate-colored nipples have my cock harder than cement. I don't have a huge package but in that building where it's a rare occasion for the ladies to see any of it all makes there day.

Size does not matter here I am not at all measure as I might be out in the world or on the guy's wards where it is always about who has got the biggest dick. Nope, back with the women they say and do things that keep me feeling like king Kong. I'm the big kahuna, the head mother fucker in charge. That's right, I felt a little guilty in the beginning when I found myself going into the staff restrooms twice within twenty minutes. Once to stroke my cock so it was as swelled as I could get it. Letting my print show knowing the ladies would always focus on that area. Then the second time would be to rub one out. Sure, there's some younger chicks there I would love to get a go at, but they were no way as needy for me as the ones in the cages were. Funny thing is I wanted them even more some days. I don't know why but it seems like the more of a reason someone has not to have something the more they want it.

I must admit I have had fantasies of punishing these women in fierce sexual ways that I'm sure may be frowned upon by some uppity types. But their opinions don't really matter to me at all. Like Danisha, for being in possession of contraband, a class one charge in our facility I love to go in her cell, tie her to four post and use her very own creations to torture her. I would lube her asshole up really nice and explore the deepest realms of her rectum as I read her the charges. She would have to plead guilty charges before I would even consider taking it easy on her back door.

Kim and Lucy, those little whores if I could have my way with them, they would both be on leashes like disobedient dogs, they would fight and argue over my dick. I would make them suck and ride my few inches till it grew another few inches. They would always be kept naked, just butt ass naked and barefoot. Alex, I know you're into all that accessory and shit, but I would give them nothing but my dick to worry about. I wouldn't mind letting you tag them with my bro. Lucy I know has a tight little cunt on her, she was caught with a shot of tequila push up in her when she came through booking, man I wish I was the guy who caught her with it. I have imagined taking her by the throat and yelling into her face "what is this?" Smacking her pretty face 'til the fear made her piss herself. "Drink it" 'til she deemed me her master in her seductive language. I would have to torment her for a long while, coaxing her exotic accent. Her well-groomed cha-cha makes her irresistible. I bet her pussy is as sweet as candy. There is just far too many of them for me to tell it all, but you get my point. My girlfriend does not mind at all, considering she gets to be the subject I release my bent-up anxiety out on. I fuck her savagely like she stole something. No seriously, I cuff her up and fuck the shit out of her after a long day of the work, they will bullshit, and cock teasers. So, I guess I take the bad with the good. The benefits are plentiful.

Alex: Ok so you are a voyeur maybe a peeper and a fan of BDSM, and you've figured how you could get paid for it, bravo! Hey as long as you're not one of those guys who rapes or is forceful to an unwilling purity, we are cool, fuck a victimized. I've done time and depending on where I would let the monster out its cage to make a decent looking female Co's. Night or day better. On the opposite side of things, I guess an inmate wouldn't mind boning one of your female co-workers to get stories from them as well as a few smokes and dirty magazines, why not. As a correction officer I'm sure you see a lot of interesting things. When I was on the inside the most fantastic thoughts of sex entered my mind. I had to put some of them down on my to do list so my lovers would know how I was feeling. Sometimes I made them worry I could hurt them with size of my dick and maybe that's why some of the mail stopped. The most important element to the inmate is phone and mail so if your lover is there behind bars, even if you are screwing around on them and most of you are, at least pick up the phone and drop a line or five. That's not too much to ask considering you're going to be sucking his dick or her pussy soon as they get back on the streets anyway, right? Anyway Kev, show some love if I ever happen to violate my probation in the future. And a big shout out to all the sexy lady cops all over the world that believe in second chances, this one is to you. And don't knock it 'til you try it people start at a safe and comfortable level that works for you it's not a competition it's about composition. YOLO (you only live once) they say, get the most out of it.

10, Jill. M, 55
Athens, GA.

Since high school I have been into romance and erotic style reads. I'm always in the market for a good read for commute. Alex, I have got to admit I was one of the women who picked up reads expecting it to be another pumped up erotica novel. Not that there's anything wrong with them at all infect those are what I usually go for, more often than not these days. That's how I came across your stuff, and I have been coming back for more since. The tales really excite me in ways I had not been in a while.

My husband and I still try to make love here and again whenever he has the time or isn't tired, he is nine years my senior, but mostly all my friends still speak of the recent day and night or great sex, actively still fucking. Generally, I can count on you to provide great stories of hot, kind of steamy sex ranging from all ages and genders so I'm not ever feeling too inappropriate for wanting that touch. I have got to admit that recently I was on the train on the way back from a conference when I picked up on of your stories and by chapter three, I had to shut it to keep me from moaning aloud. My panties were damn near soaked. The wet satin against my flesh made me feel exposed and naughty like, as the air crept up my legs under my skirt to caress my folds. I rode each bump home in silence replaying the story of the man getting out of jail and the meal on his mind was his girlfriend's asshole.

Flames kept rushing over me to the point I could not make my usual stops on my walk home. It is only a few blocks from the station, but I was afraid the young barista, when by would be welcome to feast on me if he was not too shy to ask. He just blushes and looks down my well-presented cleavage every single afternoon which I welcomed and appreciated. I always make sure I lean down over the counter pretending my eyes have gone bad. But on this day, I needed to get home to finish that chapter. And in doing so I found my bands pinching my tender nipples and rubbing on my pearl of course my husband interrupts suddenly and before he could ask, I went to my knees, and I gave him a very unexpected blow job. He had not had me do that in a while and he seemed to come alive. Thrusting into my throat and bending me over like the earlier days of our relationship. After he'd erupted all over my ass like the college jockey, I knew him to be, we even showered together, and his hands were all over me again making me giggle like a schoolgirl. Soon after, I started dinner, I just so happened to be peaking into the home office and their hubby was reading my copy of your story. So, I left him to it in fact, I let him keep it and got another copy.

Since then, we have sat side by side reading and comparing stories before fucking, yes! He's fucking me again. Thanks Alex from Jack and I. Hope you never stop writing, you're doing better than you may even realize.

Alex: I'm glad to have brought the heat back to the bedroom Jill. Ellen from that story I'm sure is somewhere blushed but grateful as well. A man is very visual, keep his eyes interested, you will be fucking forever, remember that ladies and guys tell them that before you make her feel like she is not hot anymore, and so she's getting a cup of coffee she never even drinks so the barista will drool all over her tits before your do. Damn it, fellas make the damn time keep her feeling beautiful. Couples don't be afraid to let each other know what you're interested in trying, leaving a book, this book for example tucked in the story you like, or something meant to be inappropriate so you can make your partner blush, it's healthy. for all parties involved.

No matter how old you are unless you have a medical issue sex is just going to make you good, no issue. Both male and female like to feel wanted, nothing does that like the greed of a partner's mouth, the passionate moans, and groans. Even when I'm feeling angry about something she does I can see past it when she gets dolled up to let me man handle and have my way with her. It is submissive in a sense. When I'm in the wrong or trying to earn a new toy, I aim to make her cum at least ten times in one session, you can do it with your mouths and hands fellas, the ladies already know. I just might have to create a "how to" guide for my boys that don't. being a skank or a boy toy for your mate is more than acceptable at any given time.

Husbands and wives, you own your lovers badly as they own yours, accept this and remind each other of this, it is okay. Do not take on that new age ideal "he can't, she can't tell me what to do!" It's lame and gets old quick. Appreciate and be appreciated for your love, make no mistake there are cases where the mother fucker just does not deserve it. Like my friend Kody, from Englishtown, New Jersey whose wife is one of the most beautiful women I have ever known yet he cheats and beats her. He is a drunken lonely man now, while his "pal" Ken is making beautiful Brittany cum at least four times a day, every single day. They own a wonderful restaurant together, that I won't mention since you refused to pay for the space or keep my tab open that night, you bum. You just better hope Britt never gets a craving for chocolate. Britt, mean that with all due respect.

Jack and Jill, I hope you guys never run out of passion and energy for each other. I will never stop writing and seeking out juicy, kinky tales for all my readers. The idea of making you squirm, and squirt makes me proud. I need you to keep coming back for more. Leave your panties and this novel for him ladies. Guys, this book and strawberries and cherry and cream for her. It is okay to be nasty still in this era. Love is good. Never deny your other half your body if you can help it keep it sexy.

You remember what got your partner all hot, don't you? Take it back before you ever take it down. Talk nasty to each other and keep on exploring new and exciting things. I'm a sucker for props and role playing. Even getting caught on purpose watching porn to let your partner see what it is you are interested in. Whatever it takes, do it to keep things hot cause people need that attention and if you can't get it at home, trust me there going somewhere else for it. Don't be afraid thinking he or she want for whatever reason you or they have made you believe. Unless they are just incapable, there just going to. Sorry, love has nothing to do with it.

Pamm Q 37
Lincoln, NB

Me my identical twin have not seen each other in 2 years. A week ago, I got back in town from seeing my sister in Ohio and let me tell you I will be making that trip every year. My sister Sammy has a 19-year-old son Martin, and he is a sweet kid. Well spoken and learned he has got a few tattoos that are a little to racy for my taste, but it is his skin, right? One afternoon while I was in my two-piece bikini sunbathing in the yard before school got out enjoying some shade in the blue tooth headphones not wanting anyone to see me and my fat hanging out, I kept a towel close. I have gained 40 pounds since my divorce 3 years ago and I guess I have been a little self-conscious.

Since, well anyway we were just laying there with our ear buds in, and eyes closed for a little while when suddenly something is blocking the sun out. I open my eyes to see this young ass black guy standing over me saying something., I pulled my ear plugs out to hear him. “What I asked reaching for my towel: I am sorry mis is Martin home? He asked with just a bit of sass, “No Teddy” Sammy answered for me with out rolling over to see who it was. “Ok he was speaking to Sam; but he never took his eyes off me making me feel even more self-conscious Ted” Sam mumbled still laying on her stomach. “Later ladies” he said rounding the house to the shed then leaving out the gate but not before sneaking a look at me one more time. “Sammy whispered.” When he was out of sight and hot and tightening the towel around my plum body was that boy just eyeball fucking me? “A term we use as younger girls” he’s legal to 25’ she giggled, and I bet he has got one of those BBC’s everyone talks about. What’s that I asked. It is a big black cock silly head. We laughed so hard that my tits popped out of my top. I never could keep my 40 dd’s in check.

We drank long islands and toasted both sides of our bodies before going inside. We washed up and started dinner about seven-thirty. Martin and his friend Teddy walked into the house and straight to the kitchen for bottles of water again the youngster was eyeing me. My mouth was dry all of a sudden remembering the dirty joke, so I took a sip of wine Samm had just poured us. I do not know why but my eyes went to Teddy’s crotch, and I swear I saw a bulge under his zipper. I nearly spit my wine. You, ok Martin asked patting my back. Sammy giggled out loud knowing our earlier laugh might still be on my mind and she was right. She will be ok Sammy reassured before they went out into the yard. Sam teased avoiding the question I asked.

Why is that guy always hanging around doesn't he work and at his age why is he hanging out with Martin anyway he is much older? "Sammy gulped down her glass and refilled it. Martin was dating his younger sister before she went into the Army last summer. Guess they took a liking to each other they are both into cars and he is a good kid, helps out and sticks up for Martin, Frank that shit bag sure as hell does not. "Martin's father had always been a has been I warned her about him a long time ago" Dinner in 20 guys "Sammy yelled out the back door." We set the table and dinner was served. At the table, the boys ranted about a new Nissan or something. Then I kept catching Teddy's eyes sneaking peek at my thoroughly exposed cleavage. It must have been the wine because I found myself a summer job. Then Teddy was looking dead into my eyes I felt a tingle down between my legs I had not felt in a while my nipples bead up right then I know I had too much to drink. I excused myself for a cigarette out the back door.

Made my way to the shed where the astray was and so the smoke could not wonder into the house. I took a big drag and blew out a thick cloud. "I have got to get it together" I spoke out loud. "Seems you've already got it together "Miss Pamm" the deep voice came from behind me then I knew he stalked me out there. "These things are killing people: he pointed to my cigarette. Unable to think I blurted "looking for something" I couldn't believe my ass was nervous like a schoolgirl about a guy this young. He walks over and he actually took my cigarette form my hand and takes to drags then puts it out. “Don’t tell them I smoke I only do it when my nerves are bad. This time up close his eyes undoubtedly and certainly searching my blouse low cut. “Did you lose something or just being rude young man”? I asked softly with my hands on my hips now. “I am sorry mam is there anything I can do to make amends “he was playful actually” and before pulling him into the darkness of the shed. Right away his hungry mouth went or my tits. I let him unbutton my top and let my tits spill out the silk material of my bra into his mouth. My nipples were hard as stone when the cool air met them. He sucked licked and squeezed expertly at my breast’s nipples. I let out a low moan that surprised me. My legs are weak. He must have sensed I would lose balance. He grabbed me by the ass. I had always heard that black men like big asses. Samm often told me I was all ass, and I took offence before now.

Teddy was strong his body felt hard under his shirt. I took it off and the kid, had ripped abs and muscles for arms. He pressed against me to engorge himself more into say aloud. I undid his belt and went to my knees. I could barely see his giant black dick, but my goodness could I feel it. It was heavy about the weight of my 38mm revolver easy half pound, but it was not till I had fit it into my mouth did I really realize this could be dangerous. Someone had taught him not to force a woman head down because he let me bob up and down freely on his dick, slurped a little too loudly I was greedy and just so hungry for some dick, it had been so long, and this was new. I would have never thought it would happen. Sure, I had fantasized like any other white woman in America. But now I had one a real BBC in mouth and my pussy was screaming for her turn.

Good thing I was wearing a skirt I slipped my panties to the side to rub my clit as he began thrusting face fucking me nearly choking me. I held onto his hips to keep him from going to deep. "Stand up and take this dick really quick he commanded with a low baritone voice I bent over the cooler he pulled my panties to the side and slid in slowly. I loved how he cared enough not to just impale me but then again, I think I wouldn't have minded 5 minutes of him caress my ass and slowly stretching my pussy he began to really let me have it his young energy made my pussy so wet he reached up and messaged my tits and pinched my nipples while fucking me really hard from behind so "good shit" I whispered. "You like this big black dick don't you" I looked back and shot him a look that told him the answer. I felt him throbbing inside me and that was I needed to get off. So, I bounced backwards harder and faster till I felt my own wave coming "oh shit" he covered my mouth from behind and slammed into me even harder now punishing me in a way I screamed into his hand as nearly collapse from the orgasm. "Fuck FUCK Fuck" he began really throbbing I went to my knees and let him cum all over my tits. Our eyes had adjusted to the dark and the size of his dick was still surprising me and weight made me suck him till he could take it anymore. "Now go on I said I will clean up" He scampered off like a good boy. Minutes later after another cigarette I used the front door to reenter the house pretending to be on the phone as I made my way to the shower. For the next 3 days, I let Teddy fuck me and I sucked his dick every chance we could. My sister didn't seem to notice nor did my nephew. I was worried in the beginning of our fling that we would raise an alarm or something of the sort especially when he volunteered to accompany me to the grocery store. "it's ok Miss Samm, Martins got practice and if you don't care I really don't mind helping Miss Pamm out with groceries beside I am eating most of it anyway. It is the least I can do since you refuse to take my money

I could him fainted as I approached the kitchen. "Fool I thought" hey Pamm you wouldn't mind Teddy go with you to the store so I can run to the shelter, would you? He wants to help, and we need it really quick. I FAKED A HESITATION AND FINNALLY AGREED. When we got back to the house it was empty. I had been staying in the guest room since I got to my sisters, and I was afraid I would have to pay for a new bed if Teddy kept fucking me as hard as he was on it. So, we took it to the carpeted floor. First my mouth then pussy, my tits ever my ass had Teddy's wonderful big fat black dick in it.

He suggested I record our sessions every now and again, so I did. He came on my face a new one for me, but I did not much mind it. But swallowing the warm load was more my style. I felt like such a dirty slut and was really loving every single minute of it too. We avoid too much contact when there were people around us in the house, he was over at least 3 days a week. Most of the time I was using his body I went out to get him a bottle and a hotel room or parking spot so he could do his duty and a fine job he did just fine. Here is September and my down south wanted to get back to the Midwest where I got my first peace of Chocolate and a bad sweet tooth for it. I have been watching the videos we made, BBC porn and some guys that used to frighten me from the building across the street. Things are really different now.

On the last night before I left Teddy made passionate love to me. We only spoke dirty and flirtishly when we were together. So, I am hoping he was not falling in love with me. Watching him pull me by my long-braided ponytail while commanding “throw that ass back” smacking me with his free hand to obey this order over and over is one of my go to videos. When I have my new chocolate colored 13-inch dildo out and some me time. Teddy spent a lot of time grabbing my pussy a sensation I love recreating whenever I get a chance too. There much more found love for chocolate is here to stay. Alex, just know if you ever wanted to maybe I don’t know get a few drinks and a few more of my stories I would not turn down a good offer. Would I be to forward by saying we could make some new ones if you would like. All in the name of contribution to book of course lol.

The high heels I may could get into for a night of fun with you I could do that for you. The experience suer would be something out of the world something really out of the world. At end when I had to say my goodbye, I had a feeling my sister knew something but said nothing, but twins just know what the others up to. It wasn’t till I got back did I realize my siter was no dam blind saint. She was letting me use her toy. We always played nice and shared. I wish she told me about the BBC much sooner. Thanks Sis, best summer ever! XOXO

Alex: Pamm and Sam you naughty girls. I love it. I always say "DD's and BBCs are just meant to be" I love a big fat ass, but big tits always get me going. Long hair, big tits, and a wet mouth will keep me Cumming. Shot out to Teddy for getting the ladies over to the right side of things. I have been on that mission myself. I caught that invite to Missy, make sure you really want that. Teddy is a young lad, and I will not take anything from him, but I am a seasoned stallion. You are kind of new to BBC and I should warn you that it is possible for you to get more then you bargained for. I am rough and I will work you out something serious. Even the younger women need to bring their water bottles and asthma pumps. So, I suggest you speak to your doctor first and make sure your heart is healthy enough for sex with a man like me.

My personal opinion while women who are intimidated or fear black men have been fed this by men in their family who have the same fears same goes for black people. Look slavery is over and even then, many knew about the sex on the opposite side of the spectrum. It's obvious everywhere you look that we are discovering the forbidden fruit that lay there.

The first time I had white pussy had me convinced that I had been cheating myself and shorting myself of something great. Just the contrast of our skin nearly makes me cum. We interracial couples are the set at everything from living, building, just look at our children. Perfection "stirred and not shaken" I always say. They get the best of both worlds good & bad= best you must agree if you're not one of those raciest and scared folks from either side. I love making you white women blush at my advances are nervous for those who are used to it or invite it making you ride my dick and calling me a nigger to make you feel like you're being dominated while dominating. Heavy big tits or perky tits I love them all. The colors of your eyes are so amazing. I love making you look into my eyes while you are gagging and choking on my dick. I have trained so many beautiful white girls some amazing techniques. You and your sister can use my body as much as you please. Summer or winter time. You will be at my house though. Butt naked but the heels yes, you are going to have to do that for your master. I sure you understand. Do not worry you will only be on your feet in a few bent over and squatted down positions. That is not too much is it?

I am going to admit to recording my virgins for sessions so I may watch the later and I am my own critic on detail, technique, quality, and finish. A true voyeur even watches himself. My lady you are a voyeur. You still have a way to go out but well on your way. So go on and come out of that still and explore a little. Your single I am assuming, take some time to really discover what it is you really like out there. Do not limit yourself by race or class or you will miss out on some great chances to be happy. The old generation was wrong and miserable we are to set the tune and trend for the next up.

Teddy has got the idea and so does his sister there. The tits, clits, and dicks of other races are beautiful and delicious and new. What is there to hate. Personally, every detail of white, Spanish, Asian, south African and every other light skin race out their turns me the fuck on. My brown and dark skin ladies can get it too. I guess it is really all about timing for me. The time I taught big booty Judy alone type of thing. My appetite you can say is based on opportunity not race. A juicy ass, pair of tits, pretty face, manicured nails, eyes, big lips, wide hips, things simple as cleanliness and fun to be with may have me making a woman screaming my name as I tongue fuck her holes and share my foot long dick into tight wet spaces of her precious body until we are both collapsed somewhere. Pamm makes no mistakes, there will be more for you, but can you imagine how many good orgasms you have missed with that fear you used to have? It sucks but you have time to get back some.

I cannot lie in your story I can imagine your heavy tits just swinging in the cast air in the darkness of the shed out back your sisters house and Teddy's hunger for you and Sam, when he saw you both sunbathing in the yard when you first got there. He had to be pounding at that chubby pussy of yours like no other off pure anticipation of what it would feel like no other off pure anticipation of what it would feel like to fuck the other sister. I have fucked twins before your pussies are different and to worth the drama that comes with it that is for a later story still to come. But in your case, all was well and very much appreciated by all parties that is a rare and very happily ever after if I do say so myself. Still, I wonder if Teddy had videos of your sister too stored. I know I would and your two close enough to share images. It sure sounds like it to me, and I am wondering if I could have copies. I mean I would share mine with you is all I am saying. I am so glad when the face fence is taken down letting the explore continue their journey in this very, very, short life. Cum and making cum my love "Double D's and BBCs are just meant to be.

Alex: (one of my own stories) I was dating a girl awhile back from the city of brotherly love a true tale. Angi my girlfriend has a best friend that is fucking hot, and they didn't know I knew but I knew they had been fucking each other for the past Few years. The relationship was very secretive but totally kinky. Thanks to an inside source. I didn't know how to come out and ask her for a threesome with her and her friend. Our relationship was serious, and we trust each other with everything at that point.

But admitting that I am not sure how she might feel knowing I would like to fuck her best friends lights out with her at least one time. I mean I am not ever going to cross the line without her even if we do, do it later it was just on my mind, and I felt bothered that I could always share everything with her but this one thing. Go, or no? I kept asking myself for a while. My birthday came I could help it and asked she said GO! And they did this all the time and its cool. But not if I thought it could possibly ruin what we already have. "If she is down for it will let you know Daddi "I was just going to have to find out, but it was out there.

Holding it inside just may have become an issue. Peeps who hide shit like that even if there over it do creep shit later on anyway so.... I waited and waited and waited then sure enough another year had come and gone. I thought she had either forgotten what I asked or at some point changed her mind without my knowledge but who would have guessed I was about to have a very very happy birthday.

This year my Birthday came, and my girl bought her girl over to wish me many more. That morning my lady made me my favorite breakfast after a long night toe curling sex I needed the home fries with onions and green peppers, 3 scrambled eggs and cheese, a few thick slices of bacon, a Belgian waffle served with powdered sugar and syrup and a cold cup of orange juice to recharge me for the day. She let me fuck her in ass in shower and cumming on her big tits before making my way to the bank. I took out a few grand confirmed the limo pick up at six pm then went shopping.

The afternoon I got my stylist to retwist my dreads and headed home baby girl feed me fruits and pussy for lunch. I called up my team and everyone was pretty stoked about going to the extravagant strip club I want man time without comp, anyway my theme for the night was white and gold. I got a Pretty Gang to make me an awesome all white v neck shirt with gold logo a pair of white cocaine edition Trees (those are boots) to match my jewels and grill all white gold I hate to toot my own horn but BEEEEP! I was ready for my night then my girl Lona pulled up with her girl Trish their both 5's my girl is white and Indian Trish was black maybe even Caribbean her skin brown and flawless.

Lona had good taste especially when it came to Selecting black woman. Lona's tits drove me crazy anyone who knows me knows I am an ass man, but tits were the next thing. Her hair as always colored a bright red like Charlie Baltimore. Her Halloween eyes and big lips had me taken since day one. She is a knockout. Then one day she brought around Trish, and I realized they were just the opposite. Trish was black smaller tits, but her ass is nice and oval shaped eyes and a beautiful smile, her small feet like Lona's made me want to see her in heels. I hadn't been with a black woman in a long while and I forgot why but Trish's natural beauty stood out. Seeing her and Lona together was like seeing steak served with potatoes, it was just necessary "Happy Birthday" Trish screamed reamed before giving me the usual hug and kiss, and almost right away they were playfully fondling each other as always and giggling.

Before I could complement them on their matching outfits tight skirts and tops that had cheetah prints here and there that made them look like adopted sisters my limo pulled up. Then a few of my friends pulled in, the photo shoot started, drinks and then we were on our way to the club. We picked up a few more guys in Wilmington Delaware and Chester Pennsylvania before getting there. As we rolled into the property women of all sorts seemed to just appear from all over. I felt my phone vibrate and when I checked the text "Hurry Home daddy were getting lonely and with a picture of their panties together on the floor in my room. Till this day I wish Lona would have told me what she had up her sleeve I would have gotten a real nice Hotel suite, party favors and made them a few buck richer. "They are waiting on us bro" one of my guys stuck his head back in the limo to hurry me up.

Inside the club was really fresh feeling not all muggy like most places in the city. We got the VIP and a few bottles of champaign and the sexiest girls to come up and entertain us and still I was thinking about Lona and Trisha's panties all tangled together in a stringy mesh on the hardwood floor in my room. I drank to that and then to my 30th and then to a good life and to the brothers and sisters I lost along the way. We left the club around 1:30 and by the time it was all said and done my brother had thrown up outside the window alongside the limo's doors on the highway going about 70 miles an hour, lost the stripper names sugar's number and two grand or so. But my dick stayed hard with the thought of what the fuck Lona and Trish was doing in my bed. 2:30 I pulled up to the house. I could not get out the limo quick enough.

I am filled with tequila and champaign and anticipation. I start to get undressed by the time I got there they were only in shoes and smiles "about time" Trish said "Daddi's home" Lona chimed in. They took my shirt left my chain on, took my jeans and boxers demand I war my boots. They both took one of my hands each and led me to the couch. Kisses licks at first till my cock ended up lodged in Trish's throat. I held the back of her head while me and Lana made out. They showed me nicely till I started really fucking Trish from the back as she ate Linas pretty and well shaved pussy. Trish's pussy was doing this think with her pussy muscles that made it feel like it was sucking my dick with a suction I could not resist even if I tried, not that I was. Luna knows it was because it was new pussy, I was showing her what I had, but I guess she got jealous. So, she kicked me back just a little but enough to turn me the fuck off. Two strippers had just asked me to stay the night and I am sure they wouldn't mind me fucking the living shit out of their friend. But I had to try and be thoughtful and return to this bitch's attitude and nonsense.

Poor Trish she seemed like she needed to come too, but I could not ever fake like I was still into it anymore. Ruined she fucked it all up. Lona's special talent was fucking shit up and she somehow snuck it into our bed. Eventually the memory of it and some new slut made me sure I could do better. I must admit her ability to devour my dick on demand keep me going back and forth these days. Maybe I should have trained her a little more aggressively about playing with others. Because I have had much better results with threesomes even a spectacular foursome that really took a lot out of me, to me it is where selfish and selflessness meet. When blended correctly make a mean cocktail that's cool and satisfying to the heart.

Zebra 28
Oxford, Pa

Hey Alexa, remember me? Did a few videos with you for (reacted) under my screen name. Anyway, I heard through the grape vine about your book, I am honored to have had such a great creator's cock deep inside me early in the game. Today I am doing my own thing. I own a salon too, you should come and let me twist you up and your hair too. I remember how I used to slide that big ass dick into my mouth and how yummy you have always tasted. My "pretty pink lips have always gotten wet with you on the set, I just knew you would make me keep Cumming like no other. Sucking your dick and balls, jerking your chocolate dick till I have emptied it always cross my mind. Those clips of me being your slave that kept from sold always by getting me in the "good girl" position while you would smack my creamy skin till I was raw, showing me who's the boss.

Maybe you could come tie me up that way you could take full advantage of me fucking in every opening hard and fast as you please. Slowing only to tease has always made me lose my mind. I will be a good slave for you master. Choke me hold me in position that best gets you the deepest to get me squirting hard all over that big dick. I watched a scene where you were stretching my little tight pussy then having me deep throat your dick while I finger pop my pussy and you my ass so I could cum harder than last time. So, let me ask you was I special or is that just how you fuck as well? Either way I loved screaming your name. Know that I am always ready to please “Mr. Nasty" in anyway and that mouth of yours can’t be forgotten I would like to taste my juices on your lips again that’s for sure. How about you let me know when your available I will book us a little island get away. You can repay me by kissing me from head to toe and giving me endless rounds of orgasms the best you know how, and lord knows you know how kiss up my spine as you give me back shots like you love me.

Later I will need the slut treatment maybe at random demands I can suck your dick while watching one of our old videos. Then maybe I get on my back, so you have my legs on your shoulder plowing into me, so my fat tits are smacking my face. Take my heels off and suck my toes. You have always been such a magnificent freak I am glad you’re still in the business of pleasures. Print this where you want but do respond to this ASAP I will be waiting.

Alex: yes beautiful. To all your questions I remember you I fuck that way all the time and I would love to get away with you and make “how to break a slave part 3” with you. Making you scream and squirt was awesome anytime you’re ready after December I am too. I am really grateful to have made an impression on you strong enough to have lasted in your mind so vivid?? Tats sexy as fuck. I really appreciate the love of my people have been showing me. I need your support, smarts, and sex. In return I keep putting it down or up you tell me what you’re into. I will be calling you.

www.ingramcontent.com/pod-product-compliance
Lightning Source LLC
LaVergne TN
LVHW050009180826
845678LV00022B/2974

* 9 7 9 8 3 7 3 5 9 1 6 9 0 *